Pel the patriarch

The corridor at the Hôtel de Police had at last gone quiet. The phones had stopped. Chief Inspector Evariste Clovis Désiré Pel smoothed the remaining hair sitting inconsolably on the top of his head and made for the door. There was a sound of general hilarity, enough to put Pel in a bad mood for the next twenty years. Christmas should be abolished . . .

But criminals are no respecters of religious festivities. 'One of my patients', said the doctor, 'has been beaten to a pulp. Pretty little thing, she looks like she spent the night in an abattoir. Your rapist is a madman, capable of anything, not an ordinary criminal, someone unpredictable, highly dangerous. Catch him quickly, will you? We don't want a Jack the Ripper on our hands.'

But Pel and his overworked band of detectives had something very close to it and more. 'Roger Bonnet is still missing, Claudine Bonnet is dead, Brigitte Breille was raped, Anita Tabeyse worse, and', Pel exploded, 'we've still got these ruddy robberies!'

The Burgundian *flics* were in deep midwinter and in deep with some ruthless villains. Even their own kith and kin were not immune from the violence.

Juliet Hebden's third crime novel maintains the high standard of superb characterisation and pacy narrative manifested in her own and her father, Mark Hebden's, previous books featuring Chief Inspector Pel, one of the genre's quirkiest and most likeable detectives.

The 'Pel' novels by Mark Hebden

Death set to music
(Reissued as Pel and the parked car)
Pel and the faceless corpse
Pel under pressure
Pel is puzzled
Pel and the staghound
Pel and the bombers
Pel and the predators
Pel and the pirates
Pel and the prowler
Pel and the Paris mob
Pel among the pueblos
Pel and the touch of pitch
Pel and the picture of innocence
Pel and the party spirit
Pel and the missing persons
Pel and the promised land
Pel and the sepulchre job

By Juliet Hebden

Pel picks up the pieces
Pel and the perfect partner

PEL THE PATRIARCH

Juliet Hebden

Constable · London

First published in Great Britain 1996
by Constable & Company Ltd
3 The Lanchesters, 162 Fulham Palace Road
London W6 9ER
Copyright © 1996 by Juliet Hebden
The right of Juliet Hebden to be identified
as the author of this work has been asserted
by her in accordance with the Copyright,
Designs and Patents Act 1988
ISBN 0 09 476470 0
Set in Linotron Palatino 11pt by
CentraCet Ltd, Cambridge
Printed and bound in Great Britain
by Hartnolls Ltd, Bodmin

A CIP catalogue record for this book
is available from the British Library

This must be for Ma

1

The rattling *deux chevaux* came to a noisy stop outside the small cottage; a young woman stepped out and pulled the collar of her coat up round her ears. There were icicles in the wind. It was seven in the morning, still dark, and she was tired after a long night at the hospital. Fishing in her pocket, she drew out the large key and fitted it into the lock of her grandfather's front door. She was sad he'd died but it was inevitable, she supposed – he had reached the ripe old age of ninety-three. She'd come to his lonely house to recover a treasure he'd promised her.

Stepping inside she smelt cigarette smoke. That was odd, no one had smoked in the old cottage for years. Just as fear crept into her brain the man behind the front door slipped his hand over her mouth and wrenched her left arm up behind her back. She bit him and screamed.

As she turned to run, something caught her in the mouth. It hurt, she tasted blood. Then she felt a sharper pain and heard her nose disintegrate. Staggering back, her hands to her face, she sank to her knees.

The man's boot knocked the breath from her; his fist knocked her unconscious.

She was lucky – at least she would have no recollection of what happened next.

As Chief Inspector Evariste Clovis Désiré Pel stepped out of his front door he shivered. The *Météo* had announced cold weather, record weather: it was certainly that. Pel didn't like weather, in his opinion there was far too much of it, especially at this time of year. The wind shooting down the back of his heavy overcoat confirmed his opinion. It froze his eyeballs to their sockets. It bit the end of his nose with the fangs of a tiger, it clawed round his ankles and his ears. Holy Mother of God! Winter!

'Don't stand there getting frozen, *mon cher*,' his wife said, coming up behind him and thinking he looked like an orphan standing on the doorstep. 'Off you go to your nice warm office. I'll have the fire lit for you when you come back. And', she added, *'fais attention à toi*, be careful.' There was a perfunctory kiss before Pel slid down the garden path to the stately Citroën and Madame Pel closed the door and returned to the warmth of a centrally heated house. She employed good managers in her string of boutiques so was in no hurry to leave.

To Pel's amazement the car still started first time and was willing to be reversed into the road. Too many gadgets in this thing, he thought to himself, turning the heating to Turbo. As the blasting air attempted to tear his remaining hair from its roots, he glanced in the mirror: it looked like seaweed hanging grimly on to a rock on a blustery day. Nothing changed, he sighed, but strangely his wife still seemed to love him. Miracles could happen after all. Perhaps when he arrived at the Hôtel de Police he would find the criminals on strike and he'd be able to come straight home again. No, miracles like that didn't happen. He'd arrive to be faced with the usual thousand muggings, another thousand drunk and disorderlies and possibly a couple of hundred murders thrown in for good measure. A policeman's life was monotonous. He sighed again, lit the first glorious cigarette of the day and accelerated towards the city.

The girl on the floor swam back from unconsciousness. There was a split second during which she was unaware, unremembering, then the pain struck her. She whimpered, touched her face with her fingers and wasn't surprised to find them covered in blood. She tried to sit up and in succeeding realised she was indecent. Oh God, no! It was only then that the tears filled her eyes and began rolling down her cheeks.

Daniel Darcy grabbed Kate, grinned over her shoulder at her two waiting sons, kissed her passionately and left to deliver the boys for their last day of school before the Christmas holidays and himself into the hands of Pel, his cantankerous boss, ready for another day of battling against his moods and the city's villains. As he drove he was smiling: life was all right. Pel was an old bugger but he was oddly fond of him, and Kate, well, Kate was downright delicious – even the boys were fun most of the time. Life was good, and the countryside was looking magical, covered in frost glittering in the weak morning sunlight. It was motionless and eerie, not even the peasants were out in this weather. Only policemen, school-children and the odd idiot.

The tears had stopped, now she was shaking, shaking with fear, shaking with rage, but mostly shaking with shock. Her mind cleared and she knew she must find help. Crawling to the phone she took the receiver in her bloody fingers and dialled 15, SAMU, *Service d'Assistance Médicale d'Urgence*.

Jean-Luc Nosjean tenderly caressed the swollen belly of his sleeping wife, Mijo, and crept from their apartment. He didn't like leaving her, the birth of the baby wasn't far away now; as he looked over the sparkling streets, he noticed the absence of activity but the beauty was lost on him. He hoped like hell he'd be available the day it happened. But nothing was sure in police work – maybe he should apply for a transfer to a desk job where the hours were regular and where he wouldn't risk being shot in the chest again. The bullet wound had healed but it still ached, it ached with the cold and with responsibility. Only the warmth of their bed and Mijo's loving hands stopped that. But Mijo caressed his chest less and less, she was permanently tired. Pregnancy was not what they'd expected. This wondrous event was in fact a prize bind, this last month in particular. He'd only just got used to the marital gymnastics in bed, thanks to the coaching of Darcy, and now that he was ready for anything, any time, Mijo had gone off the boil and he was left feeling randy and rejected. As he followed his breath along the icy streets he was thinking of Darcy and Kate. Darcy had been the biggest lover boy of the department, his hobby had been bed-hopping from one stunning female to the next, until he'd met Kate. Now, although he still wasn't married, he behaved as if he was – a common-law wife and two adopted sons. According to him Kate had fully recovered from her pregnancies and he'd made it quite obvious he had no need to look elsewhere, Kate was more than enough for him. Enough for Darcy – she must have recovered a thousand per cent. But her youngest was six years old. Nosjean knew he couldn't wait six years: it would dry up and drop off!

As Pel's team stood blowing on their hands in the sergeants' room the call came through from SAMU.

'Annie.' Pel looked up as he replaced the receiver. 'We've got a case of rape. You'll be needed down at the hospital while Cheriff takes a statement. Make her press charges – I doubt that she'll want to but she must. Be very gentle but firm. Cheriff,' he continued, 'she's also been badly beaten – you know the questions to ask, but take care, she's in shock. And Annie,' he added as she prepared to leave, 'try not to break anything – the last time you were in a hospital on business you left chaos in your wake.'

'I caught them though,' she replied, heading for the door with their stately Arab, Cheriff.

As the two detectives went down the corridor the Chief squeezed through the door and tried to ease himself into a chair. An ex-champion boxer, he was a large man who fitted uncomfortably into police regulation furniture but very comfortably into his position as head of the Hôtel de Police in the capital of Burgundy, the region that produces a liqueur made from blackcurrants, mustard that brings tears to your eyes and of course the best wines in France – he was well aware of his fortune. However, he was wearing a frown and a bright red woollen scarf as he sat looking at the faces in front of him.

'Heating's on the blink,' he announced, and looking round the room he realised they'd noticed. If overcoats had been removed on arrival they'd been put back on again. There was a lot of blowing on hands and lighting of cigarettes, as if that would keep them warm, he thought, poor fools. But in general they were a good crew, intelligent men who knew their jobs, and with Christmas and the New Year just round the corner he reckoned he was going to need them. It was a season of high spirits, particularly spirits that came in bottles. They produced all sorts of mayhem. Yes, he was going to need them. He was even prepared to tolerate the idiosyncrasies of Chief Inspector Pel who was sitting practising his scowl on everyone. 'Has anyone reported it?'

'Annie did first thing this morning,' Pel growled, rubbing his hands together. *'Putain de chauffage.'*

'Carry on.'

Pel sniffed, let his spectacles snap back on to his nose from his receding forehead and glared at no one in particular. 'So,' he started, 'we've now got our first grievous bodily harm and rape of the season. Merry bloody Christmas.' No one said a word, they knew their boss. 'And you still haven't solved these robberies. I want extra action, that'll warm you up a bit. It's been going on for too long and they're nasty ones. It appears that over and above the usual million problems we're juggling, we have a team of clever devils who move in after a death, when the body has been removed to the family for

11

viewing, to clear the now unoccupied house. From Debray's report, most of which is Chinese to me having come off his blasted computer, it's their *modus operandi*. And for those who don't understand Latin, like Pujol who's busy picking his nose and not listening – '

Pujol shot to attention. 'I am, Patron, *modus operandi* means the way a person goes to work – I mean his style of working, not his bike or the bus ...' He tried laughing but no one joined him. 'In police work it can sometimes be almost as good as a fingerprint, in fact – '

'Thank you,' Pel interrupted. 'Go back to picking your nose. As I was saying, a death is announced in the local papers or word gets around – you know how we, as a nation, enjoy the subject of death – then the family move in to take what they want, the television, the video machine, the stereo, perhaps an ornament or two, but leave the big stuff like the ugly old wardrobe, table and chairs, which occasionally happen to be antiques, and hey presto, a couple of days later the house is empty. No one asks questions when they see the stuff being removed – it's obvious the house is being cleared, as indeed it should be. Everyone supposes it's the family that's organised it. The removal men wear overalls, scarves, gloves, hats but it all looks pretty normal. Today it seems they may have beaten and raped a member of a bereaved family – unfortunately she must have surprised them. The SAMU chaps took an old boy out of the same house a couple of days ago, he died peacefully in hospital, but his granddaughter left the house in the same ambulance and is in a mess. So I want all the second-hand shops, *brocante* shops and antique shops covered. A list of stolen goods has been prepared so get yourselves a copy and get moving.'

'Sir,' whispered Pujol from the corner where he was hiding.

'Yes?' hissed Pel.

'What if they're taking the goods further afield, down the motorway to Marseille, up the motorway to Paris, over the border to Switzerland or west towards – '

'Thank you, Pujol.' Pel removed his glasses, lit a cigarette and stared venomously round the room. 'You have the whole of France to search for a truckload of chairs and tables, a dozen or so beds, a few freezers and a sagging sofa or two. Impossible, but you'll manage, won't you?'

As the Chief was trying to lever himself out of his chair, Pel rose and asked if there was anything else.

'Well, yes.'

'Who's that?' demanded Pel.

A hand came slowly up at the back of the crowd.

'Me,' Pujol replied, almost whispering.

'Me, who?'

'Me, Pujol, Patron.'

'Well, Pujol?' Pel blew out a gust of smoke. 'Make it quick, we're all damn well freezing in here.'

'There's been a cock disturbance reported.'

'A what disturbance?'

'Cock, sir. We've had a complaint from the owner of one of the three new houses at Talant that the cock in the farmyard behind them crows too early and wakes them up.' Pujol read rapidly from his notes. 'It's not too bad during the week, but the residents' committee wants it stopped at the weekend.'

Brochard, a farmer's son, looked up through his pale hair, a smile on his face. 'How long's the cock been in residence?'

'Forever – they've always had a cock, I understand, just as they've always had chickens, duck and guinea-fowl. It's an ordinary farm, has been for generations.'

'And how long have the houses been there?'

'Seven months.'

Brochard laughed. 'Poor bloody cock, he can't be expected to understand the townies that move in next door.'

'They also want bonfires abolished on Sundays.'

'Good God,' Brochard snorted, 'they'll be asking for the cows not to moo next.'

'They'd like them moved, their bodily functions are considered rude, they can be seen from the living-room window.'

13

Brochard laughed again and turned to Pel. 'Send Cheriff when he gets back, he's smooth enough to calm even snotty townies temporarily.' Pel was turning slowly puce.

'They don't like Arabs either,' Pujol replied quietly, not daring to look at his boss.

Pel pulled himself to his full height, which wasn't much, and glared at Pujol. 'Cheriff is French, born and brought up in our beloved Burgundy, and you don't get much Frencher than that. If he wasn't,' he added indignantly, 'he wouldn't be in the Police Judiciaire of the Republic of France.'

'He still looks like an Arab,' sulked Pujol.

'Enough!' Pel exploded, blowing cigarette smoke viciously from his nostrils. He looked as if at any minute he might burst into flames. Pujol pressed himself against the wall in the hope that he might just disappear through it. 'Under the orders of the Procureur of France,' announced Pel in a controlled voice, 'we are expected to solve crime. That is to say investigate, research, find the proof and hunt down the perpetrators. But I am sure, perfectly sure, that it does not include sorting out a piffling argument about a cockerel unfortunately waking up a few lazy idiots who want to sleep late on Sunday. That, in my opinion, and in yours now, I hope,' he went on, looking daggers at Pujol who was nodding vigorously, 'is a question of keeping the peace, maintaining law and order, *c'est à dire*, the local gendarmes can cope. Have I made myself clear?'

As he turned to leave the room he asked how on earth something so unimportant had reached the Hôtel de Police.

Pujol opened his mouth to reply, 'By phone,' but had his life saved by Darcy. 'It must have slipped through, Patron.'

'Then slip it back again fast, and Pujol, go back to your basket until you've got your brain in gear.'

As Darcy joined Pel in the corridor he was still muttering. 'Pujol the Puppy, worse than Misset.'

'Hardly, Patron.'

'Where is our fading James Bond and his dark glasses – why isn't he here?'

14

'Haemorrhoids, although he's telling everyone its ingrowing toenails. He's being operated on this morning.'

'I hope it hurts.'

'Usually does.'

'Ask the hospital if they can reprogram his brain while they're at it.'

'He's not Robocop, Patron,' Pel looked at Darcy, waiting for enlightenment, 'but he'll probably be walking like him after the op.' Darcy grinned.

Pel dismissed Darcy savagely, still wondering who the hell Robocop was, but the idea of Misset suffering did make him feel slightly better.

When Annie and Cheriff came in they'd seen both Misset, who was suffering with the help of his family, and the girl who'd been beaten up, who was suffering alone.

'Well?' Pel asked.

'Not well at all, Patron,' Cheriff replied. 'Misset looks as if he's going to burst into tears at any moment, and that was only because his wife and mother-in-law had come to see him.'

Pel switched off his growing smile. 'And the rape case?'

'They made a mess of her face,' Cheriff said.

'And the rest,' Annie added quietly.

'Brigitte Breille, thirty-five years old, nurse at Centre Hospitalier,' Cheriff read, 'unmarried, lives alone in rue de Champmaillot not far from the hospital. When she'd finished night duty she went out to her grandfather's cottage to collect a small inheritance he'd left for her hidden in the chimney. He told her about it just before dying a couple of days ago. She went to the house, unlocked the door and was attacked. She didn't see who, it was still dark. The only thing she remembers is the smell of cigarette smoke, she smelt that as she stepped inside. For the moment that's all, except that when she came round the house was empty.'

15

'Well, of course it was – you don't think they'd hang about, do you?'

'I mean empty, not a stick of furniture left.'

'So it is the same lot as before.'

'And one of them smokes.'

'Just like half of France. You'll have to get back there later and see if she can remember anything else. A lisp, an accent, a ring on the fist that hit her, aftershave. Blokes, even rapists, wear perfume. In the meantime, get the Fingerprint boys out to the cottage.'

'Already done, sir,' Annie replied.

'Is she pressing charges for rape?'

'No.'

'So, no semen sample. Annie, keep at it, she must be examined whether she likes it or not.'

'Sir, so far she hasn't had a bath, which is something. It's the first thing a rape victim usually asks for, a steaming hot bath, to wash away the filth and unfortunately the evidence. After what she's been through you must understand she doesn't want even a female doctor poking about.'

Pel looked up.

'I'm sorry, Patron, but try and understand how revolting rape is.'

'I can't, I'm not a woman,' Pel stated simply, 'I'm a policeman and I want the bastard behind bars so he can't do it again. That's why you must go back and gently but surely persuade her to agree to the examination before it's too late. If we've nothing else the semen could be our only proof – the longer we leave it the less likely it'll prove anything.'

'*D'accord*, I'm on my way.' As she left she pushed her head back round the door. 'By the way, a bloke'll be dropping in this afternoon with a dozen electric radiators. I've told him to make sure you get one.' The door banged as Cheriff disappeared behind Annie.

Pel hadn't liked Annie when she'd arrived from Belfort three and a half years ago but he had to admit she was shaping up nicely – even her violent red hair didn't disturb him any more. 'The Lion of Belfort' ... Although she was slightly tamed now, it was a nickname she carried well.

Their report, however, left him with a nasty taste in his mouth. Rape was revolting, he hoped to God it wasn't the start of something big.

2

As the light faded Pel sat scowling at the paperwork in front of him; that was the worst part of police work, pushing papers round the desk and filling in reports.

Five kilometres outside the city limits, a young woman, Claudine Bonnet, was thinking almost the same thing: the worst part of being a housewife was filling her husband's stomach. He was a tall, good-looking man and solid with it. He enjoyed traditional French food and plenty of it. She consulted her notebook, which listed the contents of her freezer in the garage, and decided after two deep gulps at the *vin cuit*, bringing back memories of Martini adverts, that *gigot d'agneau* with rosemary sprigs would go down a treat. Carefully concealing her drinking habit in the cupboard, she opened the back door and made the short journey along the garden path to the garage.

It was already dark and she wished she'd brought a torch; the night was closing in with its loneliness. As she went down the three steps to the garage she failed to see the beauty of the gently falling snowflakes. The freezer was a large one, bought just after their wedding when they dreamed of a large family, but in seven years her husband had made a lot of money but no child. They had a lovely home, a beautiful garden, she had wardrobes full of expensive clothes, but the small bedroom decorated for a baby had remained empty. As the business had grown she had become more and more lonely in a large and silent house.

It was only when she had the frozen leg of lamb clasped in

her hand and had extinguished the light in the garage that she heard a car pull up. There were voices, clear in the stillness of the evening. As she listened she stood motionless, mesmerised by the conversation between her husband and his secretary. When the car door slammed shut and the garden gate clicked open, Madame Bonnet finally stepped out of the garage into the light coming from the open back door of the house.

'*Bonsoir, chéri,*' she said cheerfully. She was looking forward to slapping his face. Having delivered her message with as much impact as she could muster, she turned on her heel and fled into the house. Leaving the back door ajar so her husband could follow her, she slammed the lump of frozen lamb down on the kitchen unit, making the cutlery rattle in the drawer below.

'Damn it,' she said loud enough for her husband to hear. 'I'm having a drink, and don't try and stop me.'

Pel rose from his desk. He was aware of something going on outside but he hadn't expected to see snow.

'Darcy!'

Darcy appeared within seconds and stood casually by the open door to the office looking like Prince Charming out of a Disney film. 'Sir!'

'It's sodding snowing!'

'I'll get on to the army and see if they can have it stopped.' Darcy grinned, flashing a brilliant row of white teeth that put the snow to shame.

'We're a few days from Christmas and it decides to snow.'

'Wonderful!' replied Darcy, thinking of Kate – he'd never rolled in the snow with her, he couldn't wait to go home.

'Wonderful? But think of it, man, in less than a week the entire hundred and fifty thousand inhabitants of this beautiful city will be drunk and disorderly and most of them sliding about in the snow. Imagine the chaos. And who'll have to clear it all up?'

'Mostly Pomereu of Traffic, the gendarmeries will cope with a bit more and no doubt we'll get the rest of it.'

'You don't seem to understand. We've already got a rape on our hands, can you imagine what it's going to be like after the celebrations?'

'Let's wait till we get there,' suggested Darcy. 'For a moment it's reasonably calm, nothing but the usual million problems. I for one am ready to put on my coat and call it a day.'

When Pel turned round to give Darcy an eloquent piece of his mind he was already gone. Perhaps he was right. Annie had been at the hospital with Brigitte Breille talking about everything but rape, trying to gain her confidence; she still hadn't had a bath but she hadn't given in to the examination either. The rest of the team had been seen to be scouring the second-hand shops, their heads down and well wrapped against the arctic conditions inside and outside. Most of them were in a hurry, specially when Pel appeared. They seemed no further forward but they certainly hadn't wasted their time. He agreed, perhaps a good night's sleep would do no harm.

As he was heaving his heavy overcoat round his shoulders there was a knock at his door and Judge Brisard came in, his portly hips swaying like an old washerwoman. Pel and the Juge d'Instruction disliked each other, so Pel was extremely displeased at the intrusion so late, he was in no mood for the pompous ass. However, he knew he was going to have to listen; a Juge d'Instruction had the right to poke his nose into Pel's affairs whenever he felt like it and to make his life difficult if he saw fit. Brisard enjoyed doing just that to Pel as often as possible.

'I was on my way home,' he said, 'and decided that you and I should confer on these robberies. One too many now, you know.'

Pel sighed and sat down again, reaching for a cigarette. 'I know.'

'This time it was rape, I believe. Not nice.'

'Particularly unpleasant,' Pel agreed, wondering how long this interview was going to take.

'What are you doing about it?'

'Everything we can, of course,' Pel replied, hanging on to his patience by the skin of his teeth.

'Tell me about it,' Brisard ordered, placing his pear-shaped posterior on a chair.

'About all of it?' Pel had an idea lurking, it was worth a try.

'But of course.'

'In that case, I'd better take my coat off and send out for sandwiches, this is going to take a good hour or two.'

Brisard glanced at his watch. He had a rendezvous with a policeman's widow that evening. It was a long-standing relationship although he piously preached family life and had a large photograph of his wife and children permanently on his desk. He considered for a moment before asking for a summary.

'You've had that,' Pel said smugly. 'I repeat, for those who weren't listening, we are doing all we can.' He rose, shuffled himself inside the immense overcoat, trying to get comfortable, and headed for the door. 'Have a nice evening with the girlfriend,' he added, seeing Brisard's mouth open to argue. For a moment they eyed each other, wondering whether war was to be declared, but Brisard didn't seem to want to continue the conversation. He left hurriedly, muttering that he'd see about the issue tomorrow.

There was already enough snow on the ground to turn the world white. Reaching the city limits, Pel lit a Gauloise from the surprisingly working cigar lighter. It might be the last of the day, he thought in panic, he'd better enjoy it. He was making an effort not to smoke at home, and as a consequence he was obliged to make up for it in the car. As he drew deeply on the cigarette, almost closing his eyes in ecstasy, he turned

21

off the main road towards his house and braked hard to avoid collision with the rear end of a slow tractor towing a large trailer full of logs.

'Damn, blast and buggeration,' he said out loud, nearly setting himself alight in the effort to brake, change gear and not drop his now smouldering cigarette. It shouldn't be allowed, he thought viciously. Its lights weren't legal, the number plate wasn't visible and there were no wing mirrors in sight. It should be reported to the police.

Fortunately for the tractor it turned left at the next junction and handicapped Pel no longer. It continued several kilometres through a small village and came to a halt in a narrow lane outside an imposing house. Two inches of snow didn't prevent the tractor from reversing into position and dumping its load to one side of the garden gate. The driver switched off the engine and made his way to the house for payment. Tapping loudly on the door, he rubbed his hands together; a good tot of whisky would help enormously, he thought.

Madame Bonnet was surprised to see him. 'Said I'd be up to deliver tonight.' The driver smiled, showing a row of black stumps that were all that remained of his front teeth. 'Me word's me word, madame, 'ere I am, snow or no snow.

''s all there, all five tonnes of nicely cut wood as ordered, 'ere's your ticket from the weighing station. Shall I take me boots off if I'm coming in then?'

Madame Bonnet turned away from the door and called up the stairs for her husband. 'Must have gone for a shower,' she muttered. 'Never mind, I'll write you a cheque.'

'Whisky'd be nice, thank you, and if you don't mind, your husband promised me cash.'

She slopped a good dose of whisky into a kitchen tumbler and ran up the stairs to ask her husband about the money. Not finding him in the bathroom she took 2500 francs out of the hiding place in the bedroom and went back down to serve herself another stout *vin cuit*.

When midnight struck she locked the back door and went

to bed, immediately falling into a deep and alcohol-laced sleep. It was only the following morning she realised that her husband had still not come home. Deciding he'd gone off to his secretary's in a huff because she'd smacked him one, she waited patiently until she was putting the leg of lamb in the oven in preparation for their informal lunch party with her brother and sister-in-law, then she rang the police.

As soon as Darcy put the phone down it rang again.

'I'm terribly sorry to trouble you, but I thought you might be interested in a few strange goings-on across the road from me.'

Darcy sighed. 'What sort of goings-on, madame?'

'Well, people coming and going in the middle of the night.'

'Perhaps they're having a party,' Darcy suggested.

'If they are, they shouldn't be. This isn't a housing estate, more's the pity – might be a bit of something to look at then. No, I'm on the edge of an industrial estate, just warehouses, you see.'

'There are deliveries at night?'

'Yes, suspicious goings-on.'

'It often happens on industrial estates. I shouldn't worry, madame.'

'But I do.'

'I'll send someone round. Perhaps you'd be kind enough to give me your name and address.'

'With pleasure! Tell me, young man, do you like the colour pink?'

Darcy had to admit he had no aversion to pink although it wasn't his favourite colour.

'Well, never mind. But when you send someone to see me make sure they like pink, and tea.'

As the line went dead Darcy stared at the phone. 'Potty,' he muttered but he made a note and dropped it into Misset's filing tray, thinking it would keep him out of Pel's hair for a couple of hours and would be gentle recuperation after his stay in Surgery.

Madame Bonnet, having reported her husband missing, expected the police to go directly to the secretary's flat and catch him in the act, that's what she'd hoped, but the police interview the complainant first so it was on her doorstep that Nosjean and Angelface Aimedieu stood stamping their feet at noon. The fact that Monsieur Bonnet had disappeared didn't count as urgent, but they'd been forced to follow up her telephone call immediately because she'd suggested he might have been murdered. That was different.

Madame Bonnet was tall, thin, pale and plain. She quite obviously made an effort with her appearance, but while it may have worked when she was in her teens the effect now was horrifying. Her heels were too high, her legs too thin, her skirt too short, her jumper too tight, her lips too red and her eyes too black, dripping gold from her ears and wearing so many rings on her fingers they looked more like knuckle-dusters. As she closed the door behind them, she smiled a thin smile and invited them to come into the dining-room.

'We're eating, you'll have to excuse us,' she said, her voice as thin as her legs. Nosjean nodded and pushed Aimedieu in front of him. He wanted to get home to his wife, at the very least he wanted to be by the phone in case she went into labour.

The main room was filled with spindly modern furniture that sat apologetically round the walls. In the centre was a robust table at which sat two extremely robust adults and a baby in its high chair. To say all three were overweight, in Nosjean's opinion, would have been an understatement. As introductions were made he tried to define where their chins finished and their necks began, but arriving at their shoulders he gave up. It looked like a Monsieur Michelin convention. The family momentarily hesitated to nod hello before continuing to dig into their plates as if they were dredging for gold.

'Come about brother-in-law?' the fat man asked, helping himself to another plateful of meat.

Nosjean composed himself, flipped open his notebook and averted his eyes. 'If your brother-in-law is called Monsieur Bonnet, Roger,' he replied, 'then yes, he's been reported missing.'

'Shacked up shagging his secretary.'

'Serge!' Madame Bonnet was looking shocked.

Aimedieu's angel face frowned. 'Why do you think that, monsieur?'

'Been rumours,' came the reply between mouthfuls.

'Such as?' continued Aimedieu.

'Such as he was having it off with her every lunch time in the back of the office.' He opened his mouth and pushed a large potato in through the orifice.

'Serge!'

The baby was gurgling gravy. Nosjean tried not to look.

'It's true, isn't it, darlin',' Serge said, turning to his obese wife, who was unable to answer having her mouth full. 'Certainly, it's true,' Serge went on. 'Seven years you've been married and not a kid in sight. We've only been at it eighteen months and look at the beauty we've produced.' Nosjean and Aimedieu preferred not to; the child was dribbling prolifically. Its mother however simpered and shovelled in some more.

Nosjean composed himself. 'Madame Bonnet, you reported your husband missing this morning at ten thirty-seven. When did you last see him?'

'Last night. He came home as usual but went out again almost immediately.'

Between mouthfuls Madame Bonnet's sister-in-law managed two words: 'Lovers' tiff.'

Madame Bonnet pushed her untouched plate away. 'As a matter of fact, yes.'

'What about this time?' her brother asked.

'His secretary, she brought him home, and I don't like that, it makes the neighbours talk.'

'Where was his own car?' Nosjean asked.

'Being serviced, actually.'

'So he was home by what time?'

'Early, around six. I was in the garage and heard him drive up.'

'Did you see him?'

'No, I heard him. The big doors were closed and I'd gone in through the small side door from the garden, I'd gone down to the freezer. I'd already switched the light off and heard the car drive up. I heard them talking and saying goodbye . . .' She trailed off, then added, 'Arranging to meet the following day.'

'A business meeting?'

'No, she was going to collect him and take him to the garage to fetch his car.'

'What happened?'

'They kissed.'

'Excuse me for asking, but how do you know?'

'I heard them.'

'Noisy kisser,' interjected the digesting brother, 'always was sloppy.'

'And then?'

'Then I went out into the garden to greet him. He was coming up the little path from the gate, and, well, I slapped him.'

'Good girl,' her brother said.

'And?' continued Nosjean, trying hard to ignore the drooling baby.

'And I turned and went into the house. I thought he had followed me but later the *bucheron* turned up with the logs and I couldn't find him anywhere. And,' she added in disgust, 'he'd left the gate open. Thoughtless, that's what he is, Princesse could have got out.'

'Princesse?'

'My little dog.' At hearing her name a small ball of fluff had alighted on Madame Bonnet's knee and was busy picking at the contents of her plate.

26

'Madame, why do you suggest he may have been murdered?'

'I have a feeling.'

Nosjean couldn't bear it any longer. 'Perhaps, madame, you would give me the name of his place of work, his colleagues' names, his secretary's name and address, and we'll take it from there.'

'Certainly,' replied Madame Bonnet, becoming business-like. 'His secretary is called Didi Dias, lives in the council flats at Tivoli, his business partner is Jacques Barthes who lives out at Talant, on the rue de la Libération, but you'll find them both in the office at 65 avenue Victor Hugo. The company is called Leisure Pleasure.'

'Appropriate,' Serge burped.

As Nosjean sought refuge in the car Aimedieu burst out laughing. 'God,' he said, 'it was enough to put you off in-laws and babies for life.'

Nosjean didn't reply, but he was frowning as he put the car into gear and drew slowly out of the snowy lane.

3

While Nosjean and Aimedieu made their escape Pel arrived at the hospital with Cheriff. Walking alongside two metres of stately Arab made Pel feel insignificant, like a mouse beside a mammoth. Even walking on tiptoe would only bring him up slightly higher than Cheriff's navel. And he was good-looking, with a thatch of curling black hair. And he didn't wear glasses. And he always looked clean and well pressed. However hard Pel tried, after thirty seconds away from his wife's tender loving care he looked as if he'd been sleeping in his clothes for months. He wouldn't have been surprised if Cheriff had bent down, plucked Pel from his feet and popped him into a passing bedpan.

Annie was sitting with Brigitte Breille when they walked into the room. Annie looked tired, Brigitte looked terrible. Most of her face was hidden behind a large plaster cast protecting her reassembled nose; both nostrils were bunged with gauze. What they could see, however, were two puffy black eyes below which her left cheek was very swollen and a livid red. She tried a smile as Annie introduced them but the fifteen stitches which held together her multi-coloured lips made her wince and she abandoned the attempt. It was impossible to tell if she'd been pretty or not – her whole face was distorted.

Pel shook her hand briefly and sat down beside her. 'Don't try and talk, just listen,' he said gently.

As Cheriff signalled for Annie to join him in the corridor Pel started speaking quietly.

'How's it going?' Cheriff asked as they stood outside the door.

28

'Horrible,' Annie replied. 'The bloke who did it deserves to be castrated.'

'There's no proof of rape yet,' Cheriff pointed out.

'No, I know, but from what she's said she was raped all right. I've seen the bruises on her thighs.'

'It's not enough.'

They fell silent for a number of minutes, waiting for Pel to finish. When he came to the door they saw the tears on Brigitte's broken face.

'She's agreed,' he said simply. 'Look after her,' and he walked away.

'Patron?'

'Annie, get in there and look after her. She'll need someone with her when they come to make the examination.' He turned to Cheriff. 'And I want no comment from you,' he growled. 'The first florist's you see, go and order a lorry-load of flowers for her. I don't suppose it'll help her in the least but it'll make me feel less of a bully.'

Nosjean and Aimedieu confirmed that the missing Monsieur Bonnet hadn't surreptitiously been to collect his car from the garage, then went on to the offices of Leisure Pleasure to interview the other partner and the secretary. A sulky young woman agreed that she had indeed delivered Bonnet home and had waited for him the following morning by the cross-roads. She disagreed, however, that there was something going on between them: on that point she was emphatic. The denial was perhaps too emphatic.

Thinking about it on their way back into the city Aimedieu smiled to himself. 'If I could act as well as her,' he commented, 'I would never have become a policeman.' He eased the car impatiently through the traffic. 'And Jacques Barthes, the partner, was a pompous little sod.'

'At least he answered our questions without blushing,' Nosjean pointed out. 'He seemed to like Roger Bonnet.

'He said he was a hard-working partner and that he

reckons his wife is either potty or permanently pickled in *vin cuit*.'

'They're both possibilities, I suppose, particularly as he's the one having the affair with the secretary – he was perfectly open about it.'

Nosjean looked worried. 'You reckon anyone stays married?' he asked finally, reaching out to clutch the dashboard as Aimedieu swept past a line of dithering cars.

Aimedieu laughed out loud. 'Well, *mon brave*, Patron Pel has managed it for the last ten-odd years. If he can manage it I would have thought anyone could.'

'Maybe his wife is mega-understanding and he doesn't mess around.'

'*Mon Dieu*! Who'd mess around with him?'

Pel was feeling depressed. Pel often felt depressed but today was worse than usual. After arriving from the hospital he'd installed himself calmly behind his desk at the Hôtel de Police and tried to organise his wife's Christmas present. He wanted it delivered on the day. Unfortunately, with the problems and the end-of-year reports they'd had to complete, it had slipped his mind and now it looked impossible. Why wasn't Annie coping with it? She was the one who'd come up with the bright idea of a Twingo. He remembered that she was sitting holding the hand of Brigitte Breille, the rape victim, who right at this moment was probably undergoing an unpleasant examination. Sighing, he blew on his fingers, turned up the electric fan heater and lifted the phone one more time. Noël! They could cancel it as far as he was concerned.

De Troq' poked his head round the door. 'Have you a minute, Patron? I've got a problem.'

Pel put the phone down and considered his request. De Troq' was a small neat man who didn't look his age. Even at thirty Pel had looked ancient. Not only that, de Troq's full title was Baron Charles Victor de Troquereau de Tournay-Turenne, he was an impoverished aristocrat who earned his living as a policeman. His title infuriated Pel; his age, his style and his neatness infuriated Pel, right down to the highly polished shoes that shone like brass; but he was a good policeman so he decided to give him the desired minute. 'But not a second more, I'm busy,' he said as de Troq' closed the door quietly behind him. 'What's the problem?'

'My mother and sister are on a cruise off the coast of America.'

'I wish I was,' Pel snorted. Impoverished aristocrats who could afford costly cruises were not, in his opinion, terribly impoverished. 'So, what's the problem?'

'My mother's been mugged.'

Pel's eyebrows shot up, almost dislodging the spectacles that were perched on top of his head. 'On a luxury cruise?'

'They were sightseeing in Brazil. Someone tried to whip her handbag. She wouldn't let go, so he hit her.'

'*Mon Dieu!*'

'She still didn't let go, even when she was on the ground and he started kicking her.'

'Didn't someone call for help?'

'Eventually, but that was after my sister clobbered him with her handbag. The mugger was out cold by then. I think she carries an avil in it by the damage she did – he's saying he'll sue her for grievous bodily harm. His lawyer has already been to see her. She hasn't actually been arrested but she wants me to go and sort things out. Mother's not a frail woman by any means, but apparently she's looking like one tucked up in bed in a ward full of strangers.'

'Can't your sister cope?'

'Normally, yes. But being Brazilians they consider her to be nothing but a slip of a girl and won't listen. Both the police and the hospital are being distinctly unhelpful. My duty as a son is to be at my mother's side and at least get them home.'

'Your duty as a policeman', Pel said stoutly, 'is here in this city.' He stubbed out his smouldering Gauloise, let his glasses fall back on to his nose and stared at de Troq'.

'Yes, Patron. But it was worth asking.' De Troq' turned to go.

'When does the plane leave?'

'Tomorrow morning at nine twenty-five.'

Pel looked down at his paperwork. 'Make it snappy. I want you back before I've noticed you've gone,' he said, turning pages.

De Troq' grinned. 'Yes, Patron. Thank you, Patron.'

While Pel was wrestling with himself, a dying cigarette, his paperwork and sorting out his wife's Christmas present, his team were slowly coming in. Nosjean was the first through his door, looking grim.

'As far as I can make out, everyone's bonking everyone else and if they're not doing that they're filling their faces with food.' He sighed. 'And the festivities haven't even started.'

'Nosjean! Pull yourself together.' Pel slammed the phone down and reached for the packet of cigarettes. It was empty. He hurled open his desk drawer. It too was empty.

Nosjean watched fascinated as his boss patted all his pockets; seeing the scowl become deeper, he suggested nipping across the road to the Bar Transvaal for another packet.

'You've got more important things to do,' growled Pel, tapping rapidly on the buttons of the intercom. 'Tell me about the Bonnet family. That's where you were, isn't it?'

Pujol's petrified face poked its way hesitantly round the door.

'Cigarettes, Gauloises, five packets,' ordered Pel without looking up. It was going to be a long evening.

Annie finally rang in at seven thirty. 'You've got your proof, Patron,' she said. 'And Brigitte Breille has got a psychiatrist with her. She's a gibbering idiot after the examination.'

'Stay with her as long as you can, Annie. Isn't there anyone to come and see her, hold her hand now it's all over?'

'No, there's no family in the area. Her parents were killed in a car crash years ago and her brother is in Brest. He has four children and doesn't want to make the journey in the snow just before Christmas.'

'She's a nurse, what about colleagues at the hospital?'

'She doesn't want to see anyone in uniform.'

'Tell them to change.'

'Same difference, Patron. Don't worry – I'll stay until she calms down.'

As Pel finished speaking to Annie, Darcy materialised in the office. 'This one's a bugger,' he said cheerfully.

'Which one? And where's Pujol?'

'Last seen running across the road in hot pursuit of some cigarettes, I believe.' Darcy grinned. 'In the meantime, why don't you attack mine?' He dropped a packet in front of his boss, who fell on them as if it was the last in the world.

'So which one's a bugger?' Pel asked, exhaling comfortably behind a cloud of smoke.

'These robberies. We've been round and round in circles and come up with exactly nothing.'

'Wonderful. Happy bloody Christmas.'

4

Christmas Eve attacked them, bringing the whole city out on to the streets in search of last-minute bargains. Children were over-excited and shouting their preferences, while parents already bankrupted by their seasonal generosity clouted them into submission. The girls at the tills were tired and wondering when they were going to be able to do their own shopping; a general air of irritability reigned throughout the city. It was no better at the Hôtel de Police. Pel had already finished a whole packet of cigarettes and was well into the second when Dr Cham came into the office with his report on the Breille rape.

'Well,' he said, 'we have a semen sample which does no good to anyone until you've got a suspect. We've got pubic hairs, nice and curly and oval in shape, red in colouring, which means the rapist was either blond, red-headed or light-brown-haired, but I'm afraid I can't tell you much else, except she was certainly raped.'

Before they'd finished their conversation the walking encyclopaedia, Leguyader, head of Forensics, joined them. He had a fat file tucked under one arm carefully labelled with the title 'Breille robbery'. Cham made a rapid exit, leaving Pel to suffer alone.

'Unfortunately,' he started, 'because public opinion doesn't agree with the idea of a national fingerprint file for everyone, all I can say is that we recovered a small piece of broken porcelain on which, having spent a long time piecing it together, we were able to determine a fingerprint. Prélat tells me that it is unknown. I give you this, hoping that eventually you will turn up the perpetrator and we will then be able to prove that he is your man. Until then I leave you with my highly researched and well-documented report on the house.'

Pel decided it was a good idea not to interrupt the man. He sat and waited for the rest, but Leguyader said no more.

'Is that all?' he asked suspiciously.

'All! Have you no idea how much I'm in demand? What I do for you is just the tip of the iceberg. We've analyses for drunken driving, road accidents, paternity cases, not to mention the industrial accidents. Forensic science isn't simply there for the Brigade Criminelle.' Pel wished he'd never asked. 'In fact,' Leguyader went on, 'I don't suppose that you're aware of it but the word "forensic" is misused the whole time. It has a Latin root, you know, and means simply "of the courts", rather like the word "alibi", which means "elsewhere". When you talk of someone having an alibi, you are incorrect, you should say that he pleads alibi.'

'Yes, thank you, professor. Is the lesson over for today?'

As he left, Pel breathed a sigh of relief and fingered the report. It could wait; had there been anything of significance Leguyader would have taken pleasure in telling him about it at length. He settled back into his chair, blissfully unaware of the chaos accumulating outside his office door.

It was four o'clock. The procession of drunks, vagrants and layabouts had begun as a trickle just after lunch, now it was like the storming of the Bastille. Pel stepped out of his office to call for Darcy and came to a halt. It looked suspiciously as if some clever little devil, a social worker probably – they had a lot to answer for, them and the Russians – had been doing a good publicity campaign. It was always bad just before the Christmas holidays, but this year ... Pel sighed and lit another cigarette, drawing the soothing smoke down into the holes in his socks – not that he had any holes nowadays, thanks to his wife, but it made him feel better to think that perhaps at any moment, because of the pressure of work, the millions of cigarettes he was forced to smoke and the thousands of kilometres he had to walk in the course of a day, his socks might just break out in holes again. At least it stopped him thinking about the possibility of breaking out in spots and being carted off to hospital. Not that there'd be a bed for him – thanks to the social worker, all the spare beds would be taken by the remaining vagrants who could muster up a cough or a limp. It was well known that down at the local nick and at the hospital three meals were served a day, the beds were passable and the showers hot for the annual sluice down. There was even television if you were good. And the lucky ones, those with a cough or a limp, they would be served by a pretty young nurse. It wasn't fair – he and his men were hard-working, honest people who bust a gut all year round for the pleasure of a few hours with the family. Pel dreaded to think about that. And a further hour in the church – Pel dreaded to think about that too. However, something had to be done about the queue into the sergeants' room, it was worse than the January sales.

He squeezed through the cluster of tramps, nearly setting two alight with his cigarette and finally giving up on it as it was knocked from his fingers. He left it to smoulder on the floor: within seconds a fight broke out to salvage it. When Pel suggested gallantly to the male that he should allow the female to have it, he demanded to know why.

'Because she's a lady, and if you were a gentleman you'd know why.'

'She ain't no lady,' the tramp retorted. 'She pees in the same bucket as me and the rest of us down at the shelter, and if you were a gentleman you'd offer 'er an 'ole one.'

Pel turned his head away as a hurricane of halitosis hit him. His breath was bad enough but they all smelt like cow dung on a hot day. They might pee in the same bucket, he thought, but I wonder if they bath in it together too. In order to disentangle himself he fished in his pocket and handed her a packet he'd pinched from Darcy, idly registering that fortunately there were only two cigarettes left; however he regretted his mild generosity two seconds later.

'Cor, thanks, darling,' the female said and planted a kiss from her stagnant lips on Pel's cheek.

Pel bolted for it. He'd let the sergeants cope on their own, they were all old enough. He, on the other hand, felt far too old and distinctly soiled.

He ran for cover in his own office as Pujol arrived panting with yet another supply of Gauloises. He snatched them from his hand and lit a cigarette, then he viciously started punching the intercom, rapping out orders to whoever replied. Had he been able to, he'd have barricaded his door.

Having pushed his papers around for hours, Pel removed his glasses and sat back. It was no good, he had to face the fact that for the next twenty-four hours it was Christmas. This meant leaving the Hôtel de Police and devoting himself to his wife's family and their festive excesses. He almost preferred drunks. He sighed. He was sure he had a cold coming, his imaginary ulcer had already started playing him up at the thought of all that he would be forced to consume, and staring venomously at the glowing end of another Gauloise he was in no doubt that lung cancer would be lurking in the New Year, if of course he survived tomorrow.

The corridors had at last gone quiet; the phones had stopped. He smoothed the remaining hair sitting inconsolably on top of his head and made for the door. Formalities had to be gone through and from the noise coming from the sergeants' room they'd already started: there was a sound of general hilarity. Enough hilarity to put Pel in a bad mood for the next twenty years. Christmas should be abolished. The season of goodwill towards men. Pel rarely felt goodwill towards anyone, and this evening less than usual. However, he told himself, his team were expecting him to raise a glass with them for a brief five minutes and they were mostly a good bunch of chaps. Even Annie Saxe, the only female member of the team, was a good chap. They deserved the honour of his presence.

'Happy Christmas, Patron!' Soppy lot, Pel muttered, fighting his way through the maze of streamers and trying to focus through the smoke. For once it wasn't his.

'Seems to be an awful lot of merriment,' he growled. 'While you're in here getting sloshed just think about all the villains out there revving up for this evening's haul. It'll be hell in here tomorrow.'

Darcy thrust a plastic beaker into Pel's hand. 'Just for once, Patron, leave them to their villainy and cheer up. You know that Christmas Day is usually quiet and the misdemeanours of this evening are not beyond the capabilities of Cheriff and the emergency team. He's in charge tomorrow, so everything'll be in order when you arrive on the twenty-sixth.'

'You're in charge then,' he scowled at Cheriff, who towered over him to his left. Standing between him and Darcy with his Disney smile he felt like an ugly little midget who hadn't been to the laundry for a long time. The only way he could get his own back was to be rotten to them. 'Don't you celebrate Christmas with all your thousands of relatives then?'

Cheriff cheerfully shook his head. 'It's against my religion.'

'Wish it was against mine,' Pel replied and took a resigned sip at the plastic mug. 'Real champagne! Who's paying?' he asked, terrified he might have been robbed by his own team.

'We had a whip round as usual and with the seasonal special offers it was only fifty francs a bottle.'

Pel studied the empty cup he was holding. 'Better give me some more then, someone's finished mine.'

While Pel's team tried to encourage him to enjoy the holiday spirit they'd smuggled into the office, a woman aged thirty-three and wearing pink dungarees crossed the asphalt and knocked on the door of the warehouse. 'Anyone there?' she called.

As the two men heard her voice they froze, looking from one to another.

'Yoo-hoo! Would you like some tea? I've got the kettle on the boil in my kitchen. Thought you might like a cup, being late and Christmas Eve and all that.'

38

The man with the beard put his finger to his lips and slid out from behind the van.

'That's nice, love, I'd nearly finished. Where do you live then?' He turned, winked at his partner and went across the road with the pair of pink dungarees.

He left her house an hour later to find his partner had finished unpacking the van.

'Okay, mate, off we go.'

'No problems with the bird then?'

'Mind your own business.' He laughed. 'Just 'cos I get the good ones and you're stuck with your missus. Look, mate, fuck off and leave me alone. We'll see each other after the holidays. I'm off for a hot bonking session in Bourg.'

The two men closed and locked the doors of the warehouse and walked to the end of the road where they parted company.

'See you then.'

'Yeah,' the bearded man called back and waited for his partner to disappear from sight. He turned smartly round and headed straight back for another cup of tea.

Cheriff arrived at the hospital at ten fifteen on Christmas morning. He was carrying a large bouquet of flowers. Brigitte Breille managed a weak smile when she saw them.

'They're from my boss to apologise for bullying you the other day,' he explained.

'I suppose he was right,' she replied, a tear welling up and spilling over. 'I just hope you put him away for a long time.'

'We're doing our best, but we'd like a bit more help from you. Have you remembered anything?'

'Well,' she said slowly, 'it was only an impression, you understand, it was dark and I lost consciousness before, well, before it happened, but I don't know, I'm not sure, maybe I just imagined it but . . .'

'Tell me anyway,' Cheriff encouraged. 'You never know.'

But as she started, the door to her room flew open. 'You Inspector Kamel, Police Judiciaire?'

Cheriff rose immediately. 'We've got another one, mate,' the ambulance man announced. 'And they're not sure she's going to make it.'

5

The twenty-sixth of December dawned bright and far too early, as usual. Pel made his way to the office sucking two Citrate de Bétaine for his indigestion and a stout Gauloise for his nerves. He was grateful it was over for another year. Being in a pensive mood but satisfied to have survived the festivities, he drove slowly and carefully, which was just as well for every other mortal out on the road that morning – Pel was a dreadful driver.

The streets were full of people making their way back to work. Since the snow was beginning to disappear the peasants were out in force on their tractors as if to prove Christmas made no difference to them. Children were out in their thousands and causing chaos on their new bicycles, proving that Christmas made a great deal of difference to them. A couple of women were having a slanging match on a street corner. It was good to see everything back to normal.

A dog shot off the pavement chased by three more; they tore across the road and disappeared down a side street. Pel congratulated himself that he'd braked rapidly and successfully avoided squashing a couple of them, but omitted to look in the rear-view mirror to see the tangle of *mobylettes*, small vans and cars piled up behind him. Oblivious, Pel gently and smoothly accelerated away; he felt he was at last getting the hang of his car.

As he pushed open the door to the Hôtel de Police his deputy followed him in, looking like a cat that had been at the cream. Damn Darcy, he thought, he's had Kate for Christmas, blast the pair of them.

'Well?' Pel growled.

'Very well, thank you, Patron,' Darcy replied happily, flashing his sparkling set of snappers. 'I hope you are well too?'

'I didn't mean that, I meant, well, what's happened since I've been gone? And since you asked, no, I'm not well, it's highly likely I'll drop dead at any minute.'

'Same as usual then?' Darcy laughed, following his boss up the stairs. He sometimes wondered why everyone who worked for him liked the old bugger.

Pel shouted after Darcy as he headed towards the sergeants' room: 'Everyone in my office five minutes ago.' That'll jiggle them a bit, he thought. It was satisfying to be in charge again.

However, when Cheriff made his report he decided he should have stayed at home.

'Another rape,' he repeated sadly. 'You'd better tell me about it.'

'Anita Tabeyse, twenty-two years old, lives with another female in a small apartment block on rue Clement Janin. She was found by a man walking his dog back from the park, she was half concealed by shrubbery. An ambulance picked her up and took her to Urgences at the hospital. She was wearing nothing but a navy blue woollen pullover, white T-shirt and bra. She was unconsciousness and hasn't come round yet. The doctors are shaking their heads. She may not pull through. Forensics and Photography were informed and went to the scene of the crime. I haven't yet been in touch with the hospital this morning. I'd like to now.'

As usual Cheriff had been short and to the point. Pel agreed he should phone through for news. It was a grim start to the day.

Apart from that, Bardolle informed him, in a controlled booming voice, only slightly louder than a fog-horn, a woman had attempted to shoot her husband while he snored after

Christmas lunch because he hadn't bought her the present she wanted. When questioned she'd said it was a joke. Fortunately she'd missed and only managed to demolish the huge television. The husband was threatening to kill her for it. Pel expected the call at any moment. However, disturbances of the peace and wild parties accounted for most of the complaints, together with pilfering and a few cases of burglary, and of course there was always Misset. Pel had to vent his anger on someone and Misset just happened to fit the bill.

'Feeling better, are you?' he asked the lounging Misset, who jumped to attention and lost his dark glasses which clattered to the floor. It was then that Pel saw the carpet slippers. 'What the hell are you wearing?'

'Slippers, Patron.'

'What the hell for?'

'My ingrowing toenails,' Misset replied, hurt that Pel hadn't remembered.

'Toenails? I thought it was piles you were suffering from? Did they do the brain transplant I ordered?' he asked savagely.

No one laughed, Pel's scowl stopped them even smirking. 'Right,' he continued, 'if that's all, you'd better get on with it, and fast.'

'Sir?'

Pel peered over his specs at the cowering Pujol. 'Not you again! What this time?'

'He wrung the cock's neck late Christmas Eve and threw it over the hedge, but the farmer found it and installed another one. Now he's threatening to wring the farmer's neck.'

Pel sighed heavily. 'Until he does, *mon petit*, it's not our problem,' he said.

'But – '

'Get out!'

As his men filed out, Misset shuffling uncomfortably, Pel looked at the long list of misdemeanours, plus the list that

43

was left over from before Christmas. Millions of them, and the end-of-year reports to get finished. He picked up a biro and started leafing through an overflowing file.

Cheriff came back through the door. 'No change, Patron, still unconscious. Brigitte Breille is being allowed home, though. I'm going over to make sure she gets there.'

'That's not necessary, Cheriff, and you know it.'

'She was about to tell me something when I was called to the second victim. I'd like to find out what it was. I don't think she'll tell me by phone.'

'I'll come with you, then,' Pel said. 'Anything but these reports.'

As they stepped out into the morning sunshine Pel noticed that the snow had almost gone; what was left lined the streets like discarded streamers, thin and grey and ugly.

'Well,' he said, 'if that was winter it wasn't too bad this year.'

Cheriff opened the door of his car. 'It's not over yet, Patron,' he replied.

'At least the snow's over for this year,' Pel insisted. 'There's nothing worse than snow.' He opened the passenger's door and stepped round it before climbing in beside Cheriff. A car sped down the street, plastering the backs of his legs with very wet dirty slush. 'Perhaps there is,' he growled, slamming the door hard enough to rattle the hubcaps.

Before escorting Brigitte Breille home Pel wanted to visit Anita Tabeyse, in the hope that she'd come round and could tell them something. But they were stopped in their tracks by a huge individual who appeared to recognise Pel.

'Of course,' Pel replied. 'Dr Boudet, yes, I remember. How are you?'

'Not pleased,' the doctor said. 'One of my patients has been beaten to a pulp, Anita Tabeyse. Pretty little thing, a bit shy but full of spirit. Now she looks like she spent the night in the abattoir.'

'We were just on our way for a progress report. Has she regained consciousness?'

Dr Boudet was not encouraging. 'Come back tomorrow,' he suggested. 'Even if she does come round she'll be in no fit state to make a statement. She has multiple contusions to the head. Her stomach, legs and buttocks were badly cut, plus extensive bruising to the genital area. Both vaginal and anal passages were penetrated. Swabs have been taken so I expect you'll be hearing from the lab this afternoon.'

'Jesus wept. What sort of animal are we dealing with?'

'He's not an animal, they're far more charming. This man's a certifiable human being,' replied the doctor seriously. 'Catch him quickly, will you – we don't want a Jack the Ripper on our hands.' He sighed heavily. 'You may find the deposit under her left thumbnail a help. Most of the others were broken but one of her thumbnails had what looked like a hair caught under it.'

Pel looked at him enquiringly, hoping to hell the hair was still there.

'Before you ask,' the doctor said quickly, 'it's been removed.'

'What fool – ' Pel started but was cut short by the sight of Leguyader marching towards them. Although he bored Pel to tears – Pel suspected that he read encyclopaedias in his spare time – he was good at his job, and he knew it. From time to time Pel was forced to admit it.

'What are you doing here? She's not dead yet.'

'No,' Leguyader said smugly, 'but she had some very interesting deposits under her left thumbnail. I'll be in touch.'

Pel turned back to the doctor, who nodded. 'I thought it would be wise before the nurses finished cleaning her up.'

'Thank you,' Pel said simply.

Brigitte Breille was standing by the window looking out on to the grey street below. 'I don't want to go home,' she told them. 'There'll be no one there and the flat'll be cold.'

'That's why we've come for you,' Cheriff explained. 'At least for the first half-hour you won't feel so lonely.'

In the car travelling east towards Brigitte's flat Cheriff tried to jog her memory.

'Oh, it was nothing,' she replied, 'a bit of useless information.'

'Let us be the judge of that,' Pel suggested.

'No, it's silly.'

'Please,' Cheriff asked, 'tell us anyway.'

'Well,' she hesitated, 'I didn't feel it, I didn't see it, but I think my attacker had a beard.'

'That's interesting, not useless,' Pel said. 'Anything else?' he added hopefully.

'No, and that was only an impression.'

'It'll do for now. But if you think of anything else, useless or silly, please get in touch with us.'

'Trouble is,' she said sadly, 'I really don't want to remember anything about it.'

'That's understandable,' Cheriff agreed. 'Annie'll be round this afternoon to make sure you're all right. She's fixing up a meeting with *L'Association des Victimes de Viole*, a group of women who have suffered the same as you. She'll tell you about it. You never know, it may help.'

'I doubt it,' she said, and so did they.

Once more struggling with his massive piles of papers, Pel was feeling harassed with yards of end-of-year reports, and sodding statistics, plus the fact that crouched in the corner of his office was a highly repugnant plumber tampering with his radiator. Having successfully sprayed a fine fountain of water right across the room to hit Pel on the forehead, he vaguely apologised, shut off whatever it was he was fiddling with and went out laughing, naturally leaving the door open. The gusts of cold air swirled round Pel's ankles, up his trouser legs, and finished by making the end of his cigarette glow lividly. It was enough to make a man worry rats.

There was a knock at his door. He glared at it. 'Yes,' he snapped. Pujol crept in. Had Pel had a couple of spare house bricks sitting on his desk he'd have hurled them at him.

'What is it?' he snapped.

'It's number two,' Pujol whispered.

'Number two what?'

'Number two cock, sir.'

'What about number two cock?'

'He shot it.'

'Get out!'

As Pujol made a lightning exit from Pel's office, twelve kilometres away Madame Claudine Bonnet was watching the weather while she stood by her kitchen window keeping a lonely vigil, waiting for the return of her husband. The sky was hidden behind heavy grey clouds, paler than that morning; it wasn't long before snowflakes began to fall. They didn't settle at first, but as night fell the ground was sprinkled white. By the time she'd swallowed a bottle of *vin cuit* and made her decision, the children in the village were leaping with glee: this time it looked like real snow. Large fluffy flakes meandered out of the heavens and came to rest one upon the other. They started talking toboggans.

Claudine hadn't talked to anyone for a long time; she was itching for a bit of conversation. She'd had one or two with herself but it wasn't the same as a real live human being. She served herself another drink, to restore her self-confidence, and taking her full glass to the phone she dialled.

Pel had almost finished one of the hundreds of end-of-year reports. He sighed, passed a hand wearily over his balding head and tried to light a cigarette but found there was one already hanging from his mouth. Shocked, he ground it to death in an overflowing ashtray. That would be the last one of the evening and very soon he wouldn't need them at all.

Every year on the thirty-first of December Pel resolved to give up smoking. Every year his wife smiled, congratulated him and knew it wouldn't last. Pel only managed not to smoke when he was asleep; by seven o'clock on the first of January he'd be in a disastrous mood and speeding towards the nearest tobacconist's.

Pel glanced at the small blue packet and slipped it into his pocket, just in case. Murderous nerve soothers, suicidal rationalisers, poisonous life savers, but he was addicted. Perhaps he'd indulge in just a couple on the way home, he was allowed to smoke in his car. Smoking in his wife's brand-new royal blue Twingo would be out of the question. However, he was pleased with himself, she had adored the new car, Renault had finally managed to find someone to deliver it on Christmas morning. Yes, he was definitely getting the hang of having a wife. Good God! He'd been married a long time now. He frowned, trying to remember how long, but the crime statistics of the year had been playing havoc with his brain all day and for the life of him the year of his marriage escaped him. How on earth his wife put up with him he didn't know, he wouldn't give himself house room. She must be a saint.

As he accelerated his windscreen wipers against the thickening snow, a snowball exploded in front of him. There were youngsters all over the place, crouching beneath the street lamps collecting handfuls of snow to hurl at their mates. He slowed right down, terrified of smearing a couple of them galloping alongside. It would have made a nasty mess of the pure white streets. It would have made a bit of a mess of the report he would be obliged to make. And it might have dented his car. They looked as if they were enjoying themselves, anyway – it would've been a shame to spoil their fun. Sentimental old sod.

As Pel crawled out of the city, terrified of getting stuck in a two-inch snow-drift, Kate went to the back door. She was surprised to have someone knocking so late. As she glanced at the clock she wondered when Darcy would be back.

'My God, what happened?' Kate stepped back in horror when she saw Marie, her next-door neighbour. Her two boys came galloping in to see what was happening and stopped in their tracks.

'He hit me.'

'Who?'

'Who do you think?' Marie burst into tears.

'Get your coats, boys,' Kate said. 'We're going out.'

'No!' Marie cried. 'Don't take me back.'

'I'm taking you to hospital, love. You need a couple of stitches and your nose putting back in the middle of your face.'

As she was loading them all into the Range Rover a ghostly figure appeared beside her.

'Where's my wife?'

'Going to hospital,' Kate replied, turning her back on him and climbing up into the car.

He held the door open, putting his pale face close to Kate's, the stubble on his badly shaved chin almost prickling her cheek.

'I want my wife,' he said menacingly.

'Hard luck,' Kate retorted.

'I'm warning you – '

Kate brought her knee up and shoved him hard in the chest with her booted foot. He rolled over on to his back. 'Warn me later,' she shouted over her shoulder as she sped off down the track.

While Marie was being looked after, Kate rang Darcy and explained.

'Get her to press charges,' he said. 'Why the hell did he hit her?'

'He'd been drinking, I could smell it on his breath.'

'So?'

'So nothing, he's a brute. I'll be home as soon as I can.'

'Okay, gorgeous, I'm leaving the office now. How about if I try and rustle something up for supper?'

When Marie was finally mended she rejoined Kate, who was waiting patiently by the door of Casualty.

'Don't look so guilty, girl,' Kate said cheerfully. 'We've been having a wonderful time playing "I Spy", you'd be surprised what the boys came up with in a hospital. I'm going to have to see their teacher about the language they're learning at school.'

Marie hung her head. 'I'm sorry.'

'What for? Forcing your husband to get drunk and bash you up?'

'It was my fault.'

'Don't be so bloody stupid.'

'It was, I should have known better.'

'It doesn't give him the right to rearrange your face.'

'You haven't asked me why yet.'

'I know why. He hit you because he's a lout and a bully.'

'But he's my husband. He was so sorry, he was crying, on his knees begging for forgiveness.'

'He was flat on his back in the snow the last time I saw him. Look, Marie, battered wives always say their husbands didn't mean to, that they are sorry and burst into tears to make you feel guilty about splitting your face open.'

'But he was,' she insisted. 'Please take me home.'

'Home! You're joking.'

'No, I'm not. I want to go home.'

Kate headed the big car towards home, incredulous at Marie's attitude. 'This wasn't the first time, was it?' she asked, remembering that when she had first met her neighbour she'd been sporting an arm in a sling. Her excuse of tripping over the cat no longer rang true.

'He's never done this before.'

'But he's bruised you a bit?'

'It was nothing.'

50

'You're unbelievable.'

'He didn't mean to, I tell you.'

'Yes, he did,' Kate insisted, 'every time he hurt you he meant to. You should press charges.'

'I can't.'

'Why?'

'He's my husband.'

'He's a bully.'

'He's still my husband.'

'Did you enjoy it? Some people do, you know. They're called masochists, and later they're called Scarface by the people in the village.'

'How dare you!'

'I dare because I care. The next time it'll be worse, it always is.'

'There won't be a next time,' Marie said adamantly.

6

Just after nine thirty Claudine Bonnet's neighbour was coming down the stairs having put three over-excited children to bed. She glanced out of the window and noticed a car parked at the crossroads. The village light was just bright enough for her to make out the shape of a man standing beside it in the ever-falling snow.

Wouldn't catch me out on a night like tonight, she thought, and went downstairs to the television and her husband.

Half an hour later the children still weren't settled. She nudged her husband who was snoring comfortably beside her. 'It's your turn,' she said and gave him a good shove in the direction of the stairs.

Coming back down after reading the riot act to his offspring he too glanced out into the night. Someone was stuck and making a hell of a noise trying to get out. Being a kind bloke he got inside his overcoat, donned his gumboots and, shouting to his wife, went out to help.

It wasn't easy. The snow was falling in bucketfuls. The driver was red in the face and in a hurry, but the car kept sliding from side to side. At last he was away, skidding down the road as if the devil himself was after him. Bad-mannered *con*, he didn't even wave thank you.

As he went back into the house, stamping his feet and brushing a couple of inches of snow from his head, the children were sleeping soundly. So was his wife. She looked cosy snuggled up in one corner of the sofa. There was a slightly erotic film simpering on the television that gave him ideas. He turned off most of the lights and moved quietly towards her.

During the early hours of the twenty-eighth of December the snow piled up in the corners of Northern France. It hadn't been forecast so when alarm clocks started ringing and the French tried to leave their homes they were surprised to find it impossible. The countryside was smothered. As the light crept over the horizon a little later a savage wind was howling, drifting the still-falling snow into the angles of streets, fields and isolated crossroads, and more dramatically bringing the motorways to a standstill. Whole villages and towns were temporarily cut off, telephone and electricity cables were down. North of the Loire River even the birds looked out from their nests and snuggled back down for the day. At eight thirty precisely the army was called out. They toiled against the blizzard for three hours, rescuing stranded cars and even the odd cow mooing dismally in a six-foot snow-drift, but at eleven thirty they put down their shovels, contacted the helicopters and left it to them to drop provisions and aid to the farms and villages that were most in need. It was impossible.

When Pel opened his eyes as dawn crept through the window he was aware of a strange blue light. The street lamp down the road usually cast a warm yellow glow that insinuated itself between the almost closed shutters. He was intrigued but pushing the shutters open was a problem for Hercules not for him. Rust, he thought optimistically, and heaving on his dressing-gown he went down to the front door. Holy Mother of God! Pel had never seen anything like it. Time for the first Gauloise! The snow filled half the doorway, it blocked entrance and exit alike. Damn Russians! It was their fault – after all, they had a hell of a lot of snow, obviously got sick of it and had sent it to France. Them and their nuclear installations. Plus of course Chirac and his damn fool explosions in the Pacific. Trust a politician to come up with something to bugger up the life of an ordinary working man. He stared bleakly at the suffocated countryside and reluctantly accepted that he wouldn't be going out today.

'Isn't it beautiful, *mon cher*?' His still sleepy wife came quietly to his side. 'Listen, not a sound.'

'Chirac should be shot,' Pel announced to his astonished wife and hurried back into the house in search of his emergency packet of cigarettes, if only he could remember where he'd hidden it.

Madame calmly closed the front door, resigned herself to the fact that she too couldn't go to work and went quietly to ease everyone's temper. A permanent state of war existed between her husband and their housekeeper, Madame Routy, and while she managed to keep the peace most of the time, today looked as if it would try the diplomacy of even Bill Clinton and his famous peacemongers. Madame Routy was to be heard crashing about in the kitchen, grinding down the iron filings for their breakfast coffee. 'Damn the politicians, damn the snow,' Pel was muttering, 'and damn Madame Routy.' He was already smoking and taking aim for the first shot with his temper.

While he silently ate his rubber croissants dunked with vigour into a bowl of steaming coffee he was thinking of the criminals of his beloved city. No Pel on the patch, they'd have a fête day. A smile filtered its way into his thoughts: if he couldn't get out, neither could they. Everyone was stuck. Bliss, but wait for the thaw, what hell that would be. However, for the moment ... His reveries were interrupted by hobnailed boots on the *carrelage* floor – there was still Madame Routy. Imprisoned in a house with a fire-eating dragon ...

Claudine Bonnet's neighbours were up with the light, their three children bouncing from room to room, demanding boots, berets, anoraks and gloves. They'd been contained for a brief moment over breakfast, then released into the silent white world outside.

'Good last night, wasn't it?' Monsieur Richard asked, feeling affectionate again.

'Mm,' replied his wife, watching three small figures hurling snowballs at each other in the garden.

'Do it again?' Richard offered.

'You were bloody cold when you came in.'

'How do you know? You were asleep.'

'Was I?' Madame Richard tilted her head teasingly.

'Yes, you were.'

'And you were still bloody cold and damp. What had you been up to?'

Richard resigned himself to conversation rather than sex. 'Helping a silly *con* out of the snow. He'd got himself stuck at the crossroads so I dashingly dug him out. Didn't even say thank you, *ni merci, ni merde*.'

'What kind of car?' his wife asked idly.

'New Saffrane, nice car.'

'Big, was it?'

'Are we talking about mine or his?' Richard sidled up against his wife hoping for a bit of horseplay.

She pushed him away. 'The car, you randy sod, the car.'

'Yes, quite.'

'Funny,' she said. 'I saw a big car there when I took the kids up. What time did you go out?'

'Oh, I don't know, around ten, I suppose. It was nearly midnight by the time we went to bed.'

'What do you think he was doing there in the snow?'

'Who knows? Who cares?'

'Strange that,' she replied, pushing her husband's hands away. 'I've told Claudine to pull her curtains, you can see her in her bedroom from the corner, you know. I've noticed coming back from the shop. She said that if they'd got the time to sit there and wait for her to undress, let them look.'

'Odd cow, that one – asking for it she is, with her miniskirts and tight jumpers, but as cold as an ice cube.'

'You'd noticed then?'

'Certainly, in between lusting after you.' He made a lurch for her and for a moment things were going merrily.

'I wonder if it was a peeping Tom,' she said suddenly and he let go, knowing that was that for the day.

Nosjean had bravely walked to the Hôtel de Police sporting snow boots, thick underwear and a woolly scarf. Debray and Brochard finally arrived from their flat around ten o'clock. Misset made it eventually, complaining of his mother-in-law, and Cheriff rode up on a horse half an hour later. Darcy borrowed Kate's Range Rover and arrived in style. The heating was still not working, like most of the city, and the men at the Hôtel de Police looked more like mountaineers wrapped up for their new expedition to the Antarctic. When the engineers were contacted naturally they claimed it was impossible to get out, so there was a lot of grumbling and rubbing of hands. Excursions were made more often to the Bar Transvaal to warm themselves up over hot chocolate, but mostly it was satisfyingly quiet. The phone rang occasionally, the odd pedestrian popped in to say hello but in general it was peaceful. Pel had rung distraught and frustrated but had been reassured that they could cope. After all, even the criminals were stuck. Nothing was happening.

Until four o'clock that afternoon.

They were just congratulating themselves on the fact that for once they'd be going home on time when two calls came in. One was from Claudine Bonnet's agitated neighbour, Monsieur Richard, who, having reflected on the problem most of the day, had been finally persuaded by his wife to report a peeping Tom. The other was from Claudine's brother saying he'd been trying on and off for a number of days and Claudine was not answering the phone.

'Perhaps her husband rematerialised and they unplugged the phone for a bit of uninterrupted making up,' Darcy suggested, wishing he could do the same with Kate.

'They say the last time they spoke to her she seemed very

depressed,' Nosjean explained. 'They're worried in case Princesse hasn't been fed.'

'Not in case his poor sister's silently committed suicide?'

Nosjean shrugged. 'I'm only repeating what I heard,' he said.

Darcy chewed on the end of a pencil briefly, gave up and lit a cigarette. 'We've got two options,' he said. 'Either we ignore it until tomorrow and we get home on time to our long-suffering wives, or we follow it up and we may not see them until next year. I know which option I prefer.'

Nosjean was tempted to start smoking again. 'Yes, but what if . . .'

'I know, we've got to follow it up,' Darcy growled. 'Phone her a thousand times and if we get no reply I expect we'll have to go and take a look.'

Nosjean flicked through the phone book looking for Bonnet's number. 'You get more like Pel every day,' he said.

At six o'clock the offices were emptying but Nosjean still had no reply. It was almost a pleasure telling Darcy, who was still at his desk in an effort to complete his statistics for the year before handing them over to his superior, Pel.

'Shit!' His reaction was to be expected. 'Come on, we'll go over in Kate's bus and let Princesse out for a pee-pee.'

The four-wheel drive car struggled valiantly through the arctic conditions. It was the only vehicle moving. Over an hour later they arrived at the crossroads and abandoned it in sight of the silent house. There were lights on downstairs so they knocked at the door, then rang the bell. There was no reply, except a faint whimpering and frantic scratching.

'Princesse,' Darcy decided, 'busting for a pee. Go round through the garden and see if you can see anything. I'll wait in case she decides to come to the door.'

Darcy stood stamping his feet and wishing he was at home in front of a roaring log fire, the kids in bed and Kate in his arms. Christmas had been good; he was wanting to repeat it.

Nosjean reappeared. 'I've been,' he said, 'I've seen and I don't like it.'

Darcy sighed, dreams of a romantic evening fading rapidly. *'Accouche,'* he said.

'The shutters at the front are slightly open,' Nosjean explained. 'I managed to get my arm in to unhook them. I've had a look into the dining-room.'

'And?'

'And there's a nasty brown stain on the floor.' He took a breath. 'Madame Bonnet's lying in it face down.'

7

So that was it. Instead of going home Darcy and Nosjean sat glumly in the Range Rover and awaited the arrival of all the necessary teams to deal with the death of Claudine Bonnet. They'd taken a look at the scene of the crime, which was grisly: the *cadavre* was in a mess, having seeped what looked like a gallon or two of blood on to the highly polished floor. They'd left it there, not touching anything, and had searched the house in case a murderer was still there – unlikely: from the smell of her, Claudine Bonnet had been dead some time – or another dead body. They looked for some evidence of what might have happened before her death, and for the bloody whimpering dog. As they'd opened the unlocked back door Princesse had fled in fright up the stairs and had hidden somewhere in one of the bedrooms. But they found nothing, not even the dog.

Forensics, Photography, Fingerprints and the medical team gathered themselves together. As they loaded the ever-ready 'murder bag' containing rubber gloves, hand lens, tape measure, straight edge ruler, swabs, sample bags, forceps, scissors, scalpels and other instruments, plus all the other necessary equipment for a murder, into the all-weather vehicles, Darcy and Nosjean sat smoking and feeling sorry for themselves.

'I thought you'd given up?' Darcy asked, suddenly realising Nosjean was dragging on his cigarette with the vigour of Pel.

'I had,' replied Nosjean, 'so don't tell Mijo.'

'How is she?'

'Fat, frustrated and fed up.'

'She ought to go and see Kate. She's been through it, might be able to cheer her up. When's it due?'

'Any minute,' Nosjean said miserably, 'and with this fucking snow Lord knows how I'm going to get her to the clinic in time.'

Darcy's eyes widened. 'I say, that's strong language from you.'

Nosjean took another deep drag. 'Well, it's true,' he said. 'We haven't got a Range Rover and we can't walk, it's at least five kilometres away. What if she started right now? Oh my God!' he cried. 'Can I ring her?'

Before Darcy had nodded, he was already punching the numbers into the car phone. After a brief discussion he breathed a sigh of relief and replaced it.

'Okay then?'

'I woke her up,' Nosjean said gloomily.

Darcy laughed and handed the unhappy Nosjean another cigarette. 'I promise I won't tell,' he grinned, 'but you look as if you need another.'

'Bloody Claudine Bonnet,' Nosjean muttered. 'What a night to get murdered.'

'I don't think she was murdered this evening,' Darcy pointed out. 'The smell in there was worse than school lavatories.'

'The heat was something else too,' Nosjean agreed.

'She must have turned it up hoping for a hot night with someone. You noticed the table was laid for two, I suppose?'

'Strange that – she reports her husband missing and a week later has been indulging in a *diner à deux*. Perhaps he'd come home.'

'Or she'd found a lover, if she didn't already have one.'

'Find her dinner guest and we'll find her murderer.'

'It may not be that simple,' Darcy pointed out.

Nosjean sighed, the last thing he wanted right now was a complicated murder case.

But that's exactly what he got.

*

Having established that she was definitely dead, the medical team stood back and watched while the photographers did their job. Once they'd finished, Dr Boudet went to work. Noting the temperature of the room, which was an astonishing twenty-eight degrees centigrade, they then set about recording the temperature of the body. Because they weren't sure if it had been a sexual attack, determining the temperature of the body in the usual way was decided against for fear of destroying valuable evidence, so a small incision was made in the abdomen, well away from the other wounds, and a thermometer was inserted. Half an hour later the thermometer was removed and the incision was marked with sticking plaster to avoid confusion. Because of the obvious wound upon it, the head was protected by a plastic bag, as were the hands, in case they could find evidence of self-defence, such as hair or skin under the nails. Hypostasis, the settling of the blood to the lowest points of the body, was noted, and rigor mortis was recorded as being complete. Boudet was frowning. The body temperature had read twenty-eight degrees; taking that away from thirty-seven and multiplying by 1.1 told him she'd been dead for just under ten hours. However, for rigor mortis to be complete she would have to have been dead for at least ten hours. He shook his head and told the waiting policemen he couldn't say when she'd died. He also told them he didn't know what had killed her. From his first examination he was tempted to say multiple stabbing, but there was broken glass in some of the wounds so he'd rather say nothing. They'd have to wait for the official report, which would take time, time to complete a full autopsy, and that was the pathologist's job.

Darcy and Nosjean both lit cigarettes, sighed and decided patience was a virtue. Pel was not going to be pleased, or very virtuous.

*

Pel was pacing the carpet at high speed the following morning. He'd slept badly as usual and was up at dawn wanting to be let out, but he was still incarcerated by snow-drifts.

'Murder,' he growled, 'and I'm stuck here unable to do a thing!'

'Darcy'll cope,' his wife said, gently pushing bowls and plates on to the breakfast table.

'That's not the point. If only they'd get their arses in gear and get rid of the snow. They can't leave me – '

The phone rang and Pel pounced on it as if it would save his life.

Darcy made his report, giving the few details that were fact but not enlarging on any hypothesis he or Nosjean had discussed. He confirmed that all the teams had finally arrived, plus Boudet, the only doctor in Dijon to own a car that would cope with the snow. 'He was still in his pyjamas,' he said, 'but was the only cheerful face amongst us. Having signed the death certificate, he stayed most of the night to ferry evidence back into the city. He even went and collected the odious Brisard who had to visit the scene of the crime before the body was moved. Took him back afterwards too. Nice bloke, Boudet.'

'Yes, I'm sure he is,' Pel hissed. 'Get me out of here, Madame Routy is driving me to drink.'

'I'll give it a whirl with the Range Rover,' Darcy suggested.

'Give it what you like, but for God's sake hurry!'

When Darcy finally arrived two hours later Pel was on the boil. Scrambling over the snow-drifts in his garden didn't cool him down; he arrived at the waiting car puce in the face, his scant hair standing on end.

Darcy silently handed him his packet of Gauloises and grinned as Pel tried to climb up into the high car whilst trying to light an urgent cigarette.

Only when Pel was seated behind his desk, puffing smoke like an unswept chimney and rapping out orders like an old-fashioned sergeant-major, did he begin to feel better. He came to a grinding halt at midday, furiously calling for Darcy.

'What's all this rubbish about having to wait for reports because of the snow?'

'Half the city can't get out of the doors.' Darcy smiled. 'The other half is using it as an excuse not to.'

'Ridiculous.'

'Patron, unfortunately we've got to accept it. There are villages on the outskirts of the city that are still completely cut off. No electricity, no phones, no water – '

'That's not my problem,' Pel interrupted. 'My problem is that I've got a dead body on my hands and I can't make any headway without the reports.'

'Reports do serve a purpose then?' Darcy asked unwisely.

'Well, of course they do, you idiot.'

'Then perhaps we'd both better use the time to finish the end-of-year reports. The Procureur will he hassling for them any minute now – for once he may not have to wait until June to get them.'

Before Pel could answer Darcy rapidly suggested the *plat du jour* at the Bar Transvaal across the road.

'The bars are still open then?'

'Apparently.'

'No, send someone across for it. I saw Misset lurking in the corridors earlier, he can go.'

'He says the snow makes his toes ache.'

'Ingrowing toenails! Hide his slippers and fit him with snow shoes or skis, give him a sled, I don't care, but tell him to get himself and his operation, whatever it was, across to the Transvaal for a beer and a hot meal for me.' As Darcy left in pursuit of Misset, Pel shouted after him, 'And tell him I've been waiting an hour already.' A smile almost appeared on his face, but as he pulled the overflowing files towards him it vanished without trace for the rest of the day.

*

Another heavy snowfall accompanied by strong winds that started early in the afternoon and went on well after night had fallen meant the Hôtel de Police became a prison for everyone inside. Camp beds were put up and the only place anyone was going that night was to eat in the bar across the road. Misset, in spite of his post-surgery aches and pains, had been given the task of keeping that track clear. He'd shovelled his way back and forth until everyone had filled their stomachs. At last it was his turn and he relaxed behind his own meal. When he'd finished he rose contentedly and stepped outside. He was going to have to start shovelling again. He'd taken far too long to eat and now even his spade was lost in a drift. Pel was standing at his window hooting with laughter as he watched poor Misset wade his way back in soggy slippers.

The following morning Pel was looking like something the cat had dragged in, but at least he had finished every report he could lay his hands on. Darcy was looking as if he'd just stepped out of a beauty parlour, clean-shaven, clothes pressed, teeth sparkling and his hair neatly combed. It was enough to make a man bite the heads off six-inch nails.

By mid-morning the snow plough had cleared the main highways and they escaped in Kate's four-wheel drive car to take a couple of hours off and long hot baths. Few people were at work. It was going to take time for the backlog to be dealt with – both Christmas and now the snow were excellent excuses – and although Pel had left shouted messages on a lot of answering machines he knew damn well there was nothing else for it but to give in and wait. Being patient was not in his nature so the next best thing was to return home to his tolerant wife and take it out on Madame Routy.

Darcy arrived home to an army of snowmen standing dripping in the clear morning sunshine. After the blanketing snow and howling winds, the sky had suddenly cleared and turned a glorious blue. The boys were out galloping about pulling toboggans and being chased by Rasputin, their monster dog. Kate was humming happily in the kitchen, getting to grips with a large lump of dough.

'Bread-making?' Darcy asked as he stepped in through the door.

Kate flung the dough on to the table and herself into Darcy's arms. 'What else am I supposed to do,' she asked, 'with the man of my life a long way from home?' Her laugh was rich and velvety. 'We've got a freezer full, they're as hard as rock and quite inedible. Heaven knows what we'll do with them.'

'Build a rockery?'

The few hours of relaxation were over far too fast. Darcy picked Pel up on his way back into the city. Very wisely Pel had decided not to drive himself; he thought it would be suicide, his wife was persuaded it could have been a massacre. As they arrived outside the Hôtel de Police they were greeted by a tall, thin and very tired-looking Dr Cham, the pathologist, hugging something hot and steaming in a small plastic mug. Beside him was the vast and laughing Dr Boudet.

'Don't know what I'd have done without Boudet,' Cham said to Pel as they went into his office. 'We were snowed in last night.'

'So were we,' Pel pointed out, not wanting to be outdone.

'Perhaps, but not with Leguyader, the walking encyclopaedia, and a roomful of dead bodies.'

'Oh, I don't know, Misset counts as three, and Pujol isn't much livelier.'

'Anyway, fortunately Boudet was snowed in with me, and fortunately amongst his medical supplies was a bottle of damn fine whisky.'

'So the red eyes aren't from tiredness and wrestling with my murder victim,' Pel said suspiciously. 'They're because of a hangover.'

'No,' replied Cham, 'they're from crying at Boudet's jokes, he's got the sickest sense of humour I've ever come across, but a hell of a way of telling them. That one about cruising up the pool . . .'

Pel sniffed; he could say a lot with a sniff. Cham stopped, deposited his file on Pel's desk and draped his long arms and legs over a chair. 'Before we start on the Bonnet murder, I should tell you that the swabs and samples we took from Anita Tabeyse confirmed that she was raped by the same man as Brigitte Breille.'

Pel scribbled something on the notepad in front of him, then looked up, waiting for information on Claudine Bonnet. Cham understood, he knew Pel of old and didn't waste time. 'She was as drunk as a lord,' he said, switching to professional mode. '3.1 grams of alcohol in her blood, what was left of it. She died from the loss of it – the blood, that is. There was a large contusion on her right temple from a hard-cornered object, there were splinters of wood present which turned out to be fragments of a log. The log was found in the hearth with the others. She had numerous lacerations to her stomach, breasts and forearms caused not by stabbing but a smashed bottle of *vin cuit* – that's what she was drunk on – ' he added, 'but those weren't enough to kill her. The real damage was done by a neat incision under her right breast which severed the innominate artery from which she bled copiously. We had difficulty in establishing the time of death because of the central heating. Her body hadn't cooled normally, so we were obliged to wade around amongst her internal organs half the night recording the changes, plus the fact that she was alcoholic hence her insides were literally pickled.' He was watching Pel who was fidgeting uncomfortably with a biro. Thinking he recognised the signs of impatience Cham went on hurriedly, 'However, we were eventually able to establish that she died at approximately midnight the night before her body was discovered.'

Pel dropped the pen and swallowed hard. 'So, she'd been stabbed to death,' he said. 'With what?'

'A very sharp instrument.'

'Oh thank you, Cham, what a brilliant deduction. Is this what you're paid for?'

'It could have been a number of things, a pair of scissors, a pointed piece of wood, a metal stake,' he pointed out calmly, 'but in fact, as I was going to say, it was a sharp, serrated-edged knife. From the traces inside the wound, which we examined in detail, it was thrust in with considerable force.'

Oblivious to the fact that Pel was turning green, Boudet continued, 'Once the knife was removed she'd have spurted blood everywhere. When we got to her she looked as if she'd taken a bath in it.'

'Open the window, Darcy, I need some air.' Pel was shakily lighting a cigarette. 'Anything else?' he asked cautiously.

'We could tell you what she'd had for supper?' Boudet suggested, warming to the subject.

'No.'

'Or what lipstick she used, mascara, eyeliner and foundation, if you like, but I don't suppose that would help?'

'No.'

'Colour of nail varnish? Perfume she was wearing? Where she bought her clothes?'

'I don't think so, thank you.'

'She hadn't had sex for a long time,' Boudet offered as they were leaving, 'so at least you know it wasn't the rapist.'

8

Nosjean joined Pel and Darcy after lunch looking very nervous and extremely worried.

'*Accouche, mon brave,*' Pel said, expecting some piece of startling information.

'They're proposing to start her off,' Nosjean replied, frowning. 'That is, if it's not spontaneous before she reaches term.'

Pel looked puzzled. 'What the hell's he on about?'

'Mijo,' Darcy translated. 'If she doesn't go into labour naturally before the date the baby's due, they'll take her into the clinic and put her on a contraction-inducing drip.'

'Oh.' Pel was still looking confused. 'You seem to know a lot about it.'

'I live with a lady who's done it twice,' Darcy explained simply.

Without thinking, Nosjean had helped himself to a cigarette from Pel's desk.

'And you're smoking again, I see.'

Nosjean nodded guiltily.

'Good man, keep it up,' Pel said happily, offering his lighter. 'Now, Claudine Bonnet, let's get to it.'

But they didn't. Leguyader entered without knocking, coughed ostentatiously and announced the previous year's death toll for lung cancer, bronchitis, heart disease and other illnesses related to smoking.

'Next time I come to give you a forensic report I'll bring my gas mask,' he finished pompously.

'Next time why don't you send one of your assistants?' Pel retorted, puffing rebelliously on a newly lit death stick.

'Because', replied Leguyader, 'you'll need me to explain it to you. Your department can't make head nor tail of my specialist findings, and without me to explain them you don't even know where to start your investigation.'

Pel was tempted to pick up the telephone directory and hurl it at him. He resisted the temptation because he was well aware that he did need Leguyader and his damn forensic report. He'd throw it at him afterwards.

'Before I start,' Leguyader said, 'I saw Prélat from Fingerprints on my way up and he asked me to give you this. The only astonishing thing they found was a number of footprints on the dining-room table, mostly badly smeared but one clear enough to identify as the victim's.'

'Dancing on the table,' Darcy said. 'I've only ever seen that done once.'

'Where was that, Inspector Darcy?' Leguyader asked, knowing the answer but hoping it might shock Pel.

'In a strip club in Paris.' Pel didn't even blink.

'Apart from that,' Leguyader went on, disappointed, 'basically they found only Claudine Bonnet's prints on the china, glasses, table and chairs. There were others around the room, none of which identify any known criminal, therefore they are presumed to be those of her husband and family. Unfortunately, they won't be a great deal of help until you have a suspect.'

'The family can be identified,' Pel said.

'It's being done, but because of the snow we've only just started. Now, more importantly,' he went on, 'my findings are a little more interesting.'

Pel sighed. 'Abridged version, if you don't mind. Because of the bloody snow we've got a lot of catching up to do too.'

Leguyader opened his copious file. Pel eyed it miserably; it was going to be a long haul. 'Firstly, we found hair and a small amount of skin tissue on the corner of a log stacked in the fireplace. It matches with that of Claudine Bonnet's head.

Secondly, in the ashes of the fire we found the blade of a knife; the handle was badly burnt but there was enough remaining for our purposes. It was bone and with the blade we have been able to identify the make.' Leguyader paused to see if Pel was impressed. He was but he wasn't going to give the forensic scientist the pleasure of showing it, he continued to look bored. 'The knife has only been on the market for a short time, made by a firm imitating the famous knives of Agiole, in the Aveyron. They went into production of the knife three months before Christmas, that is to say the beginning of October.'

'We can count,' Pel said coldly.

Leguyader was not distracted. 'This particular model has a blade engraved with three birds, a grouse, a partridge and a pheasant, to be precise. They were sold in boxes of six, designed as table knives for gentlemen hunters.'

'Are there any gentlemen hunters?' Darcy asked. 'Most of the hunters I've seen round my house are maniacs.'

'More importantly,' Pel interrupted, 'was there only one of these knives in the house, probably brought in by the murderer, or did they own a set, in which case it was – '

'There was another knife on the table,' Leguyader went on; 'the other four were in a drawer in their hideous sideboard.' He turned a page of his report before continuing. 'The knives can be bought in any shop specialising in hunting equipment and hunting accessories, as well as in a number of the more expensive shops selling cutlery. Boxes of forks and spoons are also produced in the same series.'

'But she wasn't killed with a spoon, was she? So we'll concentrate on the knives. No doubt you've put it all in your report?' Pel was wanting to cut the meeting short.

'Indeed I have and – '

'Anything else important?' Pel interrupted again.

'Read the report,' Leguyader replied, dumping it with a dull thud on the desk and turning to leave. 'If you don't understand anything ring me next year, I've got a lot to do.'

After he'd slammed the door closed Darcy turned to

Pel, who was idly fiddling with the contents of the famous report.

'You reckon it was the husband, Patron?' he asked.

'I don't reckon anything, but it's certainly a possibility.'

'But he's been missing since . . .' Nosjean added.

'So have you since your wife became pregnant,' growled Pel. 'He could have come back to murder the poor bitch. She may have been led to believe it was to make up and got herself dolled up for a nice cosy dinner. She'd been drinking, he arrives, serves her another caseload for good measure so she doesn't know what the hell's happening, he whacks her with a log and strangely returns it to the other logs, she falls to the floor on to a bottle she was holding, he wants to be sure and grabs a convenient knife from the table. Having stabbed her he chucks it in the fire and leaves her to die. But,' he added sadly, 'that's all supposition.'

'But why? Because she believed he was having it off with his secretary? That's not enough,' Nosjean said.

'You don't think so? You know bloody well people get murdered for much less,' Pel bellowed.

'Maybe she was threatening him with social ruin,' suggested Darcy, 'or to oust him from the board. His partner said both wives had shares in the firm.'

'By the way, what happened to Princesse?' Nosjean ventured.

'Who?'

'The poodle.'

Pel threw them out and lit a calming cigarette.

9

At long last the weather had settled; it was still cold, cold enough for everyone to continue complaining, but at least the blizzards were over. The countryside remained blanketed white, looking like a left-over Christmas cake, but the roads were now passable although dangerous. As teams of men and women dealt with the broken telephone lines and lack of electricity, the isolated villages began to come to life again. Trees dripped delicately and occasionally let fall dollops of soggy snow; children pulled their toboggans behind them making the most of their remaining few days of holiday. And Pel was in an evil mood.

He sat steaming behind his desk listing everything that had to be done yesterday, knowing that the more days that passed the less likely they were to crack any of their millions of cases. Everything was urgent. The detectives and their sergeants had been called in, every one of them; they were going to be working all hours from now on. Wives would complain, kids would wonder where Dad was. Pel sighed. Mijo might even give birth without her husband at her side. It was wonderful being a policeman. A new brand of plumbers had turned up, although they preferred to be called heating technicians, and they were making enough racket in the corridor with their wrenches, lengths of piping and coarse jokes to wake the dead. They had a nasty habit of barging in and out of the offices without knocking, crashing about around the radiators for a second or two and leaving without closing the door, so the warmth that Pel managed to work up with the electric heater and his Gauloises escaped every half-hour or so. It was not conducive to living in harmony at the Hôtel de Police, someone was going to have to pay.

The morning meeting was a gloomy affair. They all knew what was coming, the peace was over, war was declared. Pel was looking his grimmest. They had seen it before – *'aux armes' et cetera.* Huddled behind mufflers, swathed in thick overcoats and blowing on their finger ends, they waited for the first round of gunfire.

'No more excuses,' Pel started. 'The roads are clear enough for each one of you to get out and do business. If you get your cars stuck, continue on foot, we need results.' He banged his fist on the desk in order to emphasise what he'd said.

'Roger Bonnet is still missing,' he went on. 'Claudine Bonnet is dead, Brigitte Breille was raped, Anita Tabeyse worse, and', he shouted, 'we've still got these ruddy robberies. Darcy, who's doing what? Tell me so they know I know, it's to me they'll be answering at the end of the day.' He glared at the lot of them.

Darcy leafed through his notebook. 'De Troq' is still across the Atlantic wrestling with Brazilian red tape, he hopes to be back next week. Nosjean and I are on the Bonnet killing – '

'Why are you working together?' Pel interrupted. 'Split up and work with a junior.'

'We're working together because if Nosjean is called to the hospital I can carry on alone or delegate a junior to do the leg work.'

Pel looked across the room at Nosjean's worried face. 'Babies,' he muttered, but he agreed.

'Cheriff and Annie are dealing with the Brigitte Breille rape,' Darcy continued, 'liaising with Aimedieu and Darras who are on the other rape case, Anita Tabeyse. They are to liaise also with Bardolle and Brochard who are dealing with the robberies, in case Breille's house was cleared by the same team. Debray'll be behind his computer collating information, he's more useful there for the moment. Misset's on surveillance at the *zone industrielle*, where there have been "odd

73

goings'on", Pujol and Rigal are typing reports and answering phones, they'll be on call for anyone who needs a spare man.

'You, Patron,' Darcy finished with a smile, 'are on everything.'

As the men filed out Pel noticed Pujol dithering by the door. 'Well?' he bellowed. 'How's your cock problem?'

'He shot number three,' Pujol replied cautiously.

Pel passed a hand over his balding head and reached for his cigarettes. He'd been joking. It wouldn't happen again for a long time, if ever.

'Now the farmer is threatening to shoot the neighbour and roast him for lunch.'

'But he hasn't yet?'

'No, sir.'

Inhaling deeply to help his patience, Pel was caught in a coughing fit and while he turned an attractive shade of purple he was unable to speak. Pujol stood shuffling from foot to foot trying not to notice.

'Pujol,' Pel finally gasped, 'I think I've heard enough about your bloody cocks. Get someone impressive – Bardolle, he's big, or de Troq', he's posh, oh, no, he's not here, or Darcy, he's good-looking, or Cheriff, he's all three – to hold your hand while you explain to the cock-killing neighbour that he can't go shooting anti-social poultry. But for God's sake don't all hold hands at once or he'll think you're a bunch of carol singers that got lost in the snow.'

With that he turned back to pondering his papers. There was a hint of a smile playing round the corners of his mouth. Pujol wasn't sure if his boss was serious and Pel knew it. He hovered and hesitated, opening and closing his mouth, wondering whether he dared ask – he looked more like an anxious goldfish than a policeman. Pel switched off his smile. 'Well, get on with it,' he bellowed.

Terrified, Pujol bolted.

*

74

Boudet was standing by the bed of Anita Tabeyse when Pel came into the room with Aimedieu and Didier Darras. He smiled briefly, did the round of shaking hands, and removed his glasses almost despairingly.

'Sometimes I don't like seeing my patients.'

'Thought you enjoyed blood and guts,' Pel asked savagely.

'Not like this, I've already swallowed half a bottle of nerve pills this morning.'

'You, nerve pills?'

'*Oui*,' Boudet replied, turning back to Anita. 'It's the only way I can cope some days. I had to scrape a seven-year-old off the road this morning. Silly kid was playing on his new bicycle and slid under a lorry.'

'Will he live?'

'He's already dead. I just told his parents.'

They stared in silence for some seconds at the unconscious rape victim.

'And her?' Pel finally ventured.

'While there's life there's hope,' Boudet said softly, 'but as a professional,' he added, turning to face the detectives, 'I have to say that the longer she remains in a coma the less there is.'

'They found the rest of her clothes,' Aimedieu said. 'The lab have got them, they might turn something up.'

'When you find the man that did it, let me know.' Boudet took one last look and headed for the door. 'I'd like to rearrange his wedding tackle with my scalpel.'

Pel left the hospital to join Darcy and Nosjean on the Bonnet case. They'd radioed through to say that both the partner in the firm and the secretary were not at work, in fact not to be found anywhere, and that they were going to the Bonnet house to take another look at the scene of the crime.

As Pel slid to a halt in front of the house the next-door neighbour's wife was helping herself to the pile of logs sitting outside the gate. Guiltily she hurried off.

Pel found Darcy and Nosjean standing in the main room of the house beside the outline of where the body had been.

75

'So, having filled her with booze,' Nosjean was saying, 'he bashed her round the head with a log and stabbed her hard with a knife.'

'He obviously wanted to make certain she'd die,' Darcy replied. 'It's an odd one.'

'What are you thinking?' Pel asked.

The two men turned to see their superior. 'I'm thinking it was a very calculated murder,' Darcy said.

'You're presuming too much,' Pel snapped. 'For a start we have no idea what went on here the evening she died. There could have been an argument between her and her husband – he may, as you suggest, have come back to kill her, if he came back at all. When we find him he may be able to help us on that point. On the other hand, it may have been a third party. A peeping Tom was reported by the man next door.'

'Time to see the neighbour,' Darcy suggested.

They spent just over half an hour in the Richards' house next door, during which time they were told again how a car had been seen stuck in the snow and had been in a hurry to get away. They were also told that the Richards too had noticed Claudine dressing without pulling the curtains and for that reason they'd reported the possibility of a peeping Tom. To Pel's surprise they remembered the make of the car, having discussed it the following morning. It was a brand-new red Renault Saffrane.

Darcy contacted Pomereu of Traffic and two hours later he had the computer listing of all owners of new Renault Saffranes in Burgundy. Jacques Barthes, the remaining partner of Leisure Pleasure, was on the first page. His car was red.

10

While Pel's team were out pounding the patch and coming up with very little, a young woman not far from Darcy's home was being pounded by her husband. She'd already bounced off the wall a couple of times and was now cowering on the floor while her husband kicked savagely at her ribs. He'd been drinking again, and while she crouched there she remembered the effect Kate's foot had had on her drunken husband the last time. She waited painfully for the next onslaught. When it came, she caught hold of his foot and lifted it with all her strength. He toppled backwards and fell, cracking his head against a solid oak cupboard. Pulling herself to her feet she fled.

Kate was outside happily hanging out the washing in the hope that the pale winter sunshine might save her a bit of electricity when she heard her name being called. Looking up, she saw Marie running towards her. Immediately she called for the dog and took her neighbour into the house, slamming the door behind them.

The girl regained her breath. 'He's done it again. This time I thought he was going to kill me!'

Kate sat her at the kitchen table and extracted a small bottle of cognac from a chaotic cupboard.

'Calm down,' she said. 'Tell me all about it.'

'He's drunk, he started on the red wine at nine this morning. He's got nothing better to do, he's out of work again,' she explained.

'I don't want to hear excuses,' Kate said quietly, 'I want to hear solutions. Please don't ask me to drive you to the hospital and home again, because I'll refuse.'

'No,' Marie sobbed, 'I've had enough. I'll go home to Mum, she'll take me in. She'll drive me mad, say I told you so,' she laughed through her tears, gulping at the cognac, 'but at least I'll be safe.'

'Good girl,' Kate agreed, 'you've got to get away. Do you need a doctor?'

'No, I think I'm all right, apart from multiple bruising, as your husband would say. It must be nice to be married to a dependable detective.'

Kate didn't have time to reply; the kitchen door burst open and both women stared into the ugly face of Marie's husband, Christian.

'Where's my wife?' he screamed. 'I'm fed up with you two discussing me behind my back. You're a meddling marriage breaker,' he shouted at Kate.

Kate said nothing but sat and watched him.

'Stupid bitch, I'm hungry. When are we going to eat? Get back there and start cooking!'

'I'm not coming back,' Marie said shakily.

'Not coming back? You bloody well are.'

Kate stood up slowly. 'I think it's time for you to leave,' she said calmly. 'There's a nasty draught coming through the door and I'm not enjoying your company.'

'You and your bastard husband, fucking *flics*, always interfering. Mind your own business, I'm taking my wife home.'

'No, you're not,' Kate said emphatically.

He snorted and moved towards his wife, grabbing her by the hair. 'Who's going to stop me?' he sneered. 'You?'

'No,' Kate replied, stepping back from the table, 'I won't, but he will. Rasputin!'

The huge dog rose from beneath the table snarling through his pointed teeth.

'Wait, Rasputin, wait.'

The dog's body quivered and halted but he was still growling angrily.

'Don't force me to give the command!' Kate cried.

The man let go of his wife's hair and backed towards the door followed by an aggressive animal that looked very hungry. Once outside, he turned and ran, tripping over Kate's washing basket and leaving a trail of muddy clothes in the lane.

That evening Darcy returned home to find an extra place laid at the table and half a dozen shirts to be rewashed.

'Tell me about it,' he said to Kate.

She told him, relaxing into his arms, finally sighing and saying, 'So much for our romantic evening. Our New Year's Eve celebrations have been postponed.'

Darcy gently lifted her face towards his. 'Tomorrow, gorgeous, tomorrow. Drive her to her mother's, get the boys in bed early and we'll celebrate tomorrow.' He kissed her gently, wishing the world would go away and leave them alone.

It took most of the day to get organised. Kate had prepared a meal fit for a king. She'd already been up the lane with Rasputin to collect Marie's clothes and, to her relief, her husband was nowhere to be seen. When at last they were in the car she had second thoughts.

'Hang on a minute. I'm going to have to get someone to collect the boys from their tea party – I won't be back in time. Perhaps if I ask nicely they'll be able to stay the night.'

'Kate,' Marie said, 'please don't drive me all the way, Paris is two and a half hours away at least. You've got your own life to lead. I know you want to be with your kids and your husband this evening.'

'Daniel's not my husband,' Kate replied quietly, 'we just live together.'

'Perhaps that's the secret of being happy. Look, you've

done enough, and I'm very grateful. Take me to the station – I'll get a train. They go often enough.'

Kate was tempted, thinking of her planned evening.

The phone rang just after seven. Dreading it was Darcy to say he'd been delayed, Kate almost didn't answer. But it was Marie to say she was at her mother's and thank you. Kate breathed a sigh of relief and started talking about bathtime to her two sons.

They hadn't made much progress. Brigitte Breille was still a nervous wreck, Anita Tabeyse still hadn't come round, Claudine Bonnet was extremely dead and her husband still missing. And there were always the robberies to fill in any dull moment. Darcy, however, was whistling; he was going home to a beautiful woman and what he hoped would be a very lecherous evening. In his office he dumped a pile of files on his desk and turned to collect his coat. The phone rang. No, he thought, I'm going home, but he lifted the receiver and immediately regretted it.

'Inspector Darcy?'

'*Oui.*'

'I killed my wife.' Darcy's shoulders slumped; he reached out spontaneously for the packet of cigarettes. 'Do you hear me? I killed the slag.'

Sighing, Darcy lit up. 'Who's calling, please?'

'Shut up and listen.'

Darcy removed his coat, let it fall on the floor and listened. Pujol was hovering by the door wanting permission to leave.

'What's your wife's name?' he asked, signalling to Pujol to listen in.

'Shut up, I said. I killed the cow then I chopped her up. Yesterday the dustbin men took her away, all neatly tied up in several large plastic bags.'

Pujol's eyes widened. Darcy puffed heavily on his cigarette.

'So now she's at the rubbish dump,' the caller continued.

'Monsieur,' Darcy said, 'why are you telling me this if you won't tell me your name?'

'Because you ought to get over there and find her, she ought to be buried properly. Nice and neat in the local cemetery. Religious, she was, you see.'

'Where would that be?'

'Find my bloody wife, you cretin!'

'Yes, sir. Name and address, please.'

There was a moment's pause before the voice came again. 'I'll tell you that when you've found her,' it yelled. Then the line went dead.

Darcy looked at Pujol. '*Merde,*' he said.

'A nutter?' Pujol suggested hopefully.

'God knows. But supposing he really did make cutlets out of his wife, we can't leave her to rot on the local tip, can we?'

Pujol sadly shook his head. He hadn't been in Pel's team long, but long enough to know what was coming next.

'We'll need dogs and every spare man.'

'Most of them have gone home,' Pujol pointed out.

'Lucky buggers, it'll take all bloody night then. Get the dogs anyway, and lighting. And overcoats, scarves, gloves, hats, gas masks – and don't forget the rubber boots, since the thaw arrived everything is wet and the rubbish dump'll stink. Oh, how charming. Muster the men you can find, tell the wives we'll be late and not fit to talk to when we do turn up. Sort it, *mon brave*. I've got my own phone call to make.'

Kate was not pleased: the champagne was on ice, the smoked salmon sat with slices of lemon in the fridge, the fois gras was ready, the salad washed and dressed and the *coq au vin* simmered gently. A vintage bottle of Nuits-St-Georges sulked with her by the crackling log fire. It wasn't fair, even the two boys were in bed and fast asleep. It should have been a long and romantic evening. Instead she was sitting on her own waiting for her elusive overworked man. She looked at the bottle of wine. It looked back invitingly. 'Sod it,' she said, 'I'll have a glass.'

Towards ten o'clock she woke with a start. The house was in darkness and she could have sworn she'd heard a car, but going to the kitchen window all she saw was the night, Darcy still wasn't home. The fire was singing happily in the grate, the house was silent, so she poured herself a second glass of wine and settled down to wait.

As she finished the last chapter of her book, she shivered. It was cold. She folded her long legs underneath her and huddled herself into the corner of the sofa. Damn, damn, damn and blast. It was nearly midnight now and it still wasn't fair, the whole evening ruined because of some silly sod who'd cut up his wife. Reality hit her: she was being selfish. While she was curled up in front of a dying fire, Darcy was out in the freezing wind picking over the contents of a rubbish dump, possibly finding bits of body. He'd need lots of love and plenty of warmth when he finally turned up. Forcing her feet into her cold wellingtons, she went out to the wood-shed; after collecting an armful of logs, she stumbled back towards the door.

A van skidded in front of the house. In surprise Kate dropped the logs and flashed her torch towards the unlit van; all she saw were two eyes and a long nose. The headlights suddenly came on and after a moment's revving the wheels caught and the van was away, lurching along the lane into the night. Kate gathered up her logs and made her way wearily back to the house. Without thinking, she locked the door.

Darcy was in a temper, so was everyone else. Four of them had rummaged for hours in the rubbish dump and turned up everything that smelt and felt repulsive but there was no chopped body. A fierce wind was howling, cutting through their extra overcoats; they were wet to the knees and to the armpits and in no mood to be sociable. At long last they said a grumpy goodnight and headed for home.

When Darcy arrived he couldn't get in. He hammered

violently with his fist at the solid oak door wondering what the hell Kate was playing at. She came sleepily to open it, falling into his arms in delight. She recoiled rapidly. '*Mon Dieu*, you smell, my darling.'

'So would you,' he retorted, 'if you'd spent the evening in the local tip, picking over the remains of everyone's meals and worse, in the hope of finding a rotting corpse. And all we found', he added, 'was a load of shit.'

Kate backed off. 'Want a glass of wine?' she suggested.

'I want a hot bath and a warm bed, that's all I bloody want.'

While Darcy soaked, Kate contemplated the smoked salmon, the fois gras and the overcooked *coq au vin*. Taking the bottle of champagne out of the fridge she went upstairs.

Darcy was frowning in his bath. 'I think', Kate said, 'you need cheering up. How about a glass of champagne?'

'How about a bit of peace and something to eat?' he growled.

'How about a smile and a kiss?'

'How about . . . Come here.'

That night the temperatures dropped to a record low, three tramps died of hypothermia under the bridges of the city and in a boarded-up house with ice on the inside of the windows a young mother rose in the early hours to find her week-old baby frozen to the cot sheets.

The big Bonnet house was silent. Claudine was dead, Roger had not returned. Their neighbour Monsieur Richard eyed the pile of logs in the lane. They had frozen pipes and the temperature in the sitting-room was barely reaching twelve degrees, everyone was complaining. 'You say you've whipped a couple already?' he said to his wife.

She nodded. 'Well, they don't want them, do they?' she said, her mouth full of bread and jam.

'I reckon I'm going to whip a few more, it's damn cold in here.'

Within half an hour their fireplace was ablaze, the three

children sitting cosily in front of it watching a video. The room was beginning to feel warm. Richard slipped his arm round his wife's waist. 'I'll fetch a few more later,' he suggested, thinking the glowing logs would lend ambience to the evening ahead. But he was in for a nasty surprise.

11

It was a hand. It was definitely a hand, one frozen finger had broken off and lay at his feet looking like a sausage his wife had retrieved from the bottom of the freezer, white, slightly bent and covered in bits. He swore he'd never eat chipolatas again. But if it was a hand, he said to himself, it must be attached to an arm, which would be attached to a body. He ran back to the house to throw up.

Pel arrived at the house with Darcy and Nosjean to be greeted by a crowd of highly excited children. Temporary lighting had been set up as dusk fell and the log pile was sealed off from the public. Slowly the experts were removing the wood to reveal the body.

'Is he dead, sir? Sir, is he dead?'

'I think it's highly likely,' Pel replied coldly. He liked children in general but there were times when he would have preferred their absence.

'What did he die of?'

'I couldn't say.'

'Was he murdered?'

'Who is it?'

'Is there any blood?'

Before Pel had time to become exasperated, a piercing female voice shouted an order from her back door and three of the children ran for cover. He followed the voice to the Richards' house.

'I believe your husband found the body?' he enquired politely.

'Yes, come in,' she replied pleasantly. 'Give me a moment to beat the kids into submission and I'll go and drag him from the bathroom. Something seems to have disagreed with him.'

It was Roger Bonnet with a very large dent in his head. Monsieur Richard was incapable of leaving the lavatory, but his wife went out and told them who it was.

'So he hadn't scarpered with his secretary after all,' she said. 'Poor devil, what a way to go, he must have been cold.'

Madame Casteou, the other Juge d'Instruction, arrived. Pel liked her. She came, she saw and she left; unlike Brisard, who would have made their life hell for days on end, she let the police get on with their job. She was young, uninterfering and dynamic, able to grasp the situation in seconds and leave the experts to make their reports – besides, she was very pretty, which always helped.

Pel was puzzled. When he read the lab's preliminary report through it was evident that they were having difficulty in determining the time of death, as with his wife: she'd been cooked, he'd been frozen. He'd been frozen, partly thawed and refrozen. The freezing had halted all the usual putrefaction, but close examination of the changes in blood and internal organs at the autopsy had given them their clues, and finally after extensive exploration of blood cells and skin tissue they were able to determine that he had in fact been dead for a number of days before being discovered. The lab was also unable to say what had caused the considerable fracture to his skull: it hadn't killed him but had eventually caused his death, rendering him unconscious under five tonnes of logs.

'Génial,' Pel said, viciously stubbing out a cigarette and reaching for another. He glared at Darcy and Nosjean. They reached for cigarettes too. 'We have specialists who can't do their job because of the weather, and weather than renders our specialists almost useless. Well, we'll just have to carry on with what we've got. Someone did for both of them. Who?

Why? Find the bloody partner. Solve something, this is ridiculous.'

The remaining snow looked grubby and sad; the temperature rose during the day with bright sunshine in clear blue skies, but at night it still plummeted well below zero. Special shelters had been set up all over France for those without homes but there were always a few who incredibly wanted to stay outside wrapped in newspapers, huddling together in cardboard boxes for protection against a freezing wind. The streets of the cities were almost empty, the countryside was motionless except for the odd car pulling a trailer of logs, quickly filled in the surrounding woodlands. Families opened up fireplaces that had been cold for years. Only the plumbers were pleased – everyone needed them for burst pipes and central heating that couldn't cope. They crashed about happily at the Hôtel de Police, infuriating Pel with their noise and gossip, but he was even more infuriated when they packed their bags and clattered off down the stairs to a so-called emergency. He suspected the emergency was a simply a stiff whisky in a bar down the road and he was tempted to tell the gendarmes to get their breathalyser equipment ready.

Annie had introduced Brigitte Breille to the Rape Victims' Association and had gone with her the first time. She was amazed to find that almost half of its members had never been to the police. She was also surprised to find Darcy's address listed.

She found him struggling over some incorrect statistics.

'They don't tally,' he announced unhappily, pulling his jacket collar up. 'Sometimes I think we need a ruddy accountant to sort them out for us.'

'Why's it so cold in here? What's happened to your electric heater?'

'Pel pinched it, his exploded.'

Annie burst out laughing. She sat down and asked him about the addresses she'd found.

'Well, I haven't been raped,' he said, 'it can't be Kate, so it must be Marie, the girl who lives at the end of the lane. It's the same address as us. Ring Kate and ask her.'

'It was a long time ago,' Kate replied to Annie's question, 'when she was sixteen, but she joined the association to see if she could be of help to other victims. Trouble is, she'll be joining the Battered Wives too if she comes back.'

The moment Kate had put the phone down, it rang again.

'Marie, I was just talking about you – how are things?'

'I need some stuff from the house. My mother's driving me mad, so I've found a small flat with a friend here in Paris, but it's unfurnished. We thought that if the coast's clear we'd come and load the necessary – after all, I paid for most of it.'

'Sounds good to me. I suppose you've got a couple of good burly blokes to help you load?'

Marie laughed. 'I have indeed. I'm going to live with one of them, known him all my life, he's as solid as an oak sideboard and about as dependable. And', she added, 'he's got two small kids – I'm going to look after them.'

'Fine,' Kate said cautiously. 'I hope it works out well for you, but for God's sake be careful. I've been out with Rasputin to give him a run and I've never seen anyone at the house. There are no lights lit at night according to Darcy, so I reckon you'll be okay. Pop in on your way back and we'll have a drink to celebrate.'

Darcy was late again. This week he'd been late every evening; Kate was beginning to wonder if they'd ever have a bit of uninterrupted time together. When he finally drew up in front of the house, he was tired and fed up. Kate's sons withdrew to the television recognising the signs of irritability as Kate poured him a stiff drink. They were just easing into a little recuperative conversation when they heard voices outside. It was Marie back with her two burly blokes, whom she

88

introduced as Pierrot and Janneau. Darcy thought he recognised Pierrot but let it pass.

'That didn't take long,' Kate said, closing the door. 'You only went down about half an hour ago, you can't have loaded very much.'

'We didn't load anything,' Pierrot said unhappily. 'She's been robbed.'

'The house is empty,' Marie explained.

Darcy wanted to leave: he'd come home and found he was still at work.

'*Cambriolé?*' he asked, knowing the answer.

'Looks like it, nothing left but my husband's espadrilles. I'm not surprised – they smell like a ripe old Camembert.'

It was only after the police teams had left and Marie and her two burly friends had at last said goodnight that Darcy and Kate were alone. It was well after eleven o'clock but Darcy was sitting checking his corrected statistics while Kate chewed her thumb behind a new book. Her long legs were curled up under her on the sofa, her full breasts rose and fell gently beneath a navy blue pullover. Suddenly he wanted to reach out and touch the long dark hair that fell and curled over her shoulders, he wanted to take her beautiful face in his hands and kiss her first on the lips, then in the nape of her neck, then . . . He watched her from behind his file. She gave him a warmth he'd never felt before, a need to come home, a pleasure to wake up, a *joie de vivre*. He loved her, it was aching in him – if anything should happen to her, hell's teeth, what would he do? What would happen to the boys? Go back to their titled father in England, he supposed. He couldn't let that happen – strangely enough, he loved them too. Life would be very quiet without them, and desperately dull. He'd just got to marry her, he'd ask her when; he knew she'd shrug and say that they were fine the way they were, no need to rush things, but he decided to ask her anyway.

'Kate,' he said softly, getting up from the chair by the fire and turning to poke at a smouldering log.

As she lifted her head the log decided to break violently in two and shower the stone floor with burning embers.

'Bugger,' he said, starting to sweep them together, 'bugger, bugger and double bugger.'

'Yes, darling, and the same to you,' she laughed and rose to help him. 'Fancy a brandy?'

'I fancy you.'

'And a brandy?'

'I'll settle for both.'

'I'll go and get a couple more logs then.'

'What for? The fire'll keep going for a while yet.'

'I was rather hoping to keep it going much longer.' The tilt of her head and a wicked smile told Darcy what she meant. 'You get the brandy, I won't be a moment.'

He poured generous nightcaps and placed them on the low table beside the sofa. Under one of the glasses he put a scrap of paper on which he'd simply written 'I love you'.

When Kate came back through the door with an armful of wood, he closed it behind her and helped her stack the logs in their place; then, taking her in his arms he noticed she was frowning. He kissed her anyway and for a second her face relaxed, enjoying the moment, but as he led her to the brandies the frown returned.

'What's up? Kissing not what you had in mind?'

'No – yes – of course it is,' she said, thinking hard, 'but there's something else.'

He passed her a glass of brandy, silently cursing because had she taken it from the table herself she would have seen his message. As she tasted the strong liquid, she smiled, touching his cheek with her free hand.

'I'm sorry,' she said, 'but out there in the wood-shed with my torch I just remembered something.'

'Forget it and come here.'

'But it might be important.'

'Not as important as us.'

'A van came up the lane, or at least it was going back down when I saw it.'

'I don't care, I'm lusting after your body, you're driving me mad, stop talking about vans and start talking about sex.'

'I saw a man's face,' she said, frowning again. 'He looked nasty. The night you were called out to the rubbish tip – remember, I'd locked the door? That's why.'

Darcy had had enough. He took the glass from her hands and pulled her towards him.

'Darcy! I'm telling you – '

His mouth quietened hers while he slid his hand under her jumper and, finding the button of her jeans, expertly started undoing it.

The following morning, while Kate continued to clear up the evidence of the night before and ran round in circles trying to get two small boys ready for their first day back at school, Darcy was already in Pel's office.

'You believe this van to be the one the robbers removed the furniture with?' he asked.

'It's likely,' Darcy replied. 'The cottage is at the end of the track. No one comes past our house unless they're going there.'

'Or they're lost,' Pel suggested.

'That happens in the summer with the tourists who take any turning to find a good picnic spot, but not at this time of year.'

'Fair enough, it's likely then,' Pel agreed. 'So tell me, what was this van like? Ordinary size, ordinary colour, four wheels and a hooded driver?'

'Patron, my witness is Kate, not our usual village idiot. It was white or pale beige, she thinks more likely pale beige, it could have been a Traffic, it was certainly that size. It was in a hurry to leave once they realised they'd been seen. It arrived on side lights, then skidded away on headlights when she

91

flashed her torch into the driver's face. As he turned to drive away she caught him in profile; he had a prominent chin and large nose and probably a close-cropped beard. She reckons she might just recognise him, but that's only a "might". She flashed her torch at the number plate as the van skidded away and went straight in to write it down.'

'Miracles will never cease,' Pel said, impressed.

'The miracle is that she managed to find the bit of paper in the chaos in the kitchen.' Darcy passed him the piece of torn paper. Unthinkingly Pel turned it over and saw 'I love you' written on the other side.

'I love you too,' he said, in danger of smiling, 'but it won't get you extra days off. Go and fax this number to everyone and ask your delightful wife to come and look at our villains' photo album.'

'She's not my wife,' Darcy corrected.

'Well, it's about time she was,' Pel growled, already immersed in the files on his desk. 'In the meantime get on with the fax.'

While Kate was searching unsuccessfully through the mug shots, Sarrazin, the freelance journalist, was fidgeting in Pel's office. He'd been waiting half an hour and was ready to make them pay – his time was precious. At last Pel came through the door with Darcy and an extremely attractive woman. It wasn't often they had such beauties at the Hôtel de Police; in his surprise Sarrazin forgot to be surly and rose politely to greet them.

'Oh God, not you,' Pel said, shuffling behind his desk and searching for cigarettes.

Sarrazin was still sizing up the lovely lady hoping he might get a chance to interview her. Surely she wasn't a criminal? No handcuffs, therefore she must be a witness, but to what? Sarrazin would find out if it killed him, then he'd spend a long interesting hour in her company with perhaps a bottle of bubbly, letting her tell him the story. For once he wasn't only interested in a scoop for the newspaper.

'Sarrazin!' Pel bawled. 'Stop drooling! You're enough to put me off my Gauloise, and I shouldn't bother with the smooth talk, *elle est prise*. This, my friend, is Darcy's wife.'

Sarrazin stopped drooling. 'I'm not your friend, Pel, and if I remember correctly, and I always remember correctly, Darcy isn't married.'

'He's almost married,' Pel replied, puffing vigorously on his cigarette.

'But not quite.'

'As good as.'

'Nothing's as good as, if you're not married you can still play the game.'

Kate laughed. 'I'm very flattered but not interested,' she said, smiling. 'Darcy's my man and I don't want to change him, thank you.'

'Yet,' Sarrazin insisted.

'If we give you a story,' Darcy suggested, 'will you go away?'

'Maybe.'

'If you don't I might just be forced to do you a bit of grievous bodily harm. You heard the lady, now leave her alone.'

Darcy related the story and the description of the van to Sarrazin who, while he wanted to linger, eventually gave in and left, promising it would be published in the local paper the next day.

'Seen this?' he said, handing over the newspaper. 'The *flic*'s wife finally remembered and she made a note of our number.'

'Reckon she remembers your face too? It says nothing here about it, but she got a good look at you.'

'No problem, I'll shave my beard off and we'll change the number plates on the van.'

'What about Madame Darcy?'

'We'll sort her out this afternoon.'

*

93

The sun was shining over the bare winter countryside; it was warm through the windscreen of the old Renault 4. Once again Darcy had pinched the big four-wheel drive car and Kate was left with the wreck. It didn't matter, all she had to do was collect the boys from school a few miles away, then turn round and come home again -- anyway, she was fond of the old car, it made such a nostalgic noise. When she'd lived in England, occasionally she'd hear a tinny old French car in the town where she was shopping and stop and sigh, thinking of France. How she'd longed to live here and she'd finally made it; escaping from a disastrous marriage, she'd packed her bags and her boys into her Bentley and fled to France. The old Bentley she'd left for her French father in his falling-down château; they went together, he said, and besides he loved the car that made the peasants stare wide-eyed as he cruised round the Tarn with her mother beside him. Kate had replaced it with the Range Rover but since Darcy had pinched it because of the bad road conditions she contented herself with the old Quatrelle. Her rotten husband she'd replaced with a dashing detective. Life was never what you expected; certainly she hadn't expected to move to Burgundy and set up home with Darcy, not when she'd first met him, it was de Troquereau who'd been more likely. But she didn't regret it, Darcy was an intelligent man, a terrific stepfather and a wonderful lover. She hoped and prayed it would last forever but having had one failed marriage she still wasn't ready to go through it again. Perhaps she should; she smiled, thinking of Darcy and their life together. It made her sing.

She slowed down as she approached the village. The football ground was five metres below her on the right but the entrance to the school was just round the corner and you never knew if there'd be a child on a bike leaving in a hurry who wasn't looking. Before she reached the corner she was knocked off the road.

Suddenly she was out of control, careering towards a plane tree. Wrenching at the wheel, she missed the tree but her

94

front wheels hit an exposed root. Then she was flying, turning over in the air as the playing field rushed up towards her. Then the explosion as the old car hit the ground, the tearing metal, the smashing glass. Then silence.

12

Anita Tabeyse had come round. The medical staff at the hospital were wise enough to let her rest a couple of hours before calling the police. A psychiatrist was present when Pel arrived with Annie Saxe and Didier Darras; he warned them to go easy as she was in no fit state to answer a barrage of questions and he wasn't at all sure she was ready to remember anything. And he wished to remain in the room while the police officers made their enquiries.

Pel sighed. Thank God for psychiatrists, he thought, if it weren't for them we could all behave normally.

'*Entendu,*' he said and sat meekly on the hard wooden chair beside Anita's bed. She was frail, her face badly bruised, her pale hair in disarray. Looking out from swollen eyes she tried a feeble smile and abandoned it immediately, wincing because of the stitches in her cheek.

'Mademoiselle,' Pel started quietly, 'I appreciate you have suffered enormously, but there are one or two questions I must ask you.'

She nodded faintly.

'Do you remember', he went on, 'anything about your attacker, the smallest detail? Was he tall? Short?'

She closed her eyes and, lifting a bandaged hand, cautiously wiped away a tear.

'That's enough,' the psychiatrist said.

'I've only just bloody started!' Pel hissed.

'I'll give you two more minutes, then you leave her alone and come back tomorrow.'

Pel needed a cigarette. He knew the doctor had the authority to have them thrown out, he also knew that the poor girl was still in shock and likely to remember nothing at all. He had to think, choose his words carefully. For that he needed a cigarette. A spontaneous reaction to his thoughts moved his hand to a pocket, withdrew a Gauloise and placed it calmly between his lips.

'You can't smoke in here!'

Pel rapidly removed the cigarette and was ready to crush it back into his pocket when a tiny trembling voice from the bed stopped him.

'May I have one, please?'

Pel looked at the doctor, who looked at the patient, then shrugged his shoulders, accepting the inevitable.

Anita took the cigarette in her shaking fingers and waited for Pel to give her a light. He did so, lighting a second cigarette for himself. For a moment they puffed silently.

'He smoked,' Anita whispered.

'The man who did this to you?'

'Yes, he stopped me and asked for a light, I had a cigarette in my hand.' She frowned, recalling with pain what had happened. Didier quietly took out his notepad and poised his pencil.

'He must have seen it and thought I could give him a light. I couldn't be bothered to rummage around in my bag for the *briquet*, so I gave him my cigarette.' She inhaled deeply, closing her eyes, then sighing out a river of smoke. 'He thanked me and turned to go and I set off towards my flat again. Then he said something I didn't hear properly so I stopped and turned round. He asked me if I'd like a drink. I said, "No, thank you, I'm tired, and want to go home." He said, "How about later?" I said, "No, I want to go home, take a shower and watch the telly." He said, "We could watch the telly together after a drink." I said, "No thank you," and turned to walk away. He shouted, "I suppose a fuck's out of the question?" and I started running.'

No one moved, only the smoke from the two cigarettes

continued curling silently towards the ceiling. 'He caught up with me and grabbed my arm. He said, "I asked you if you'd like a fuck." I said, "No thank you, I wouldn't." He laughed and said, "What a shame, because you're going to get one anyway," and he pushed me towards the bushes on the side of the road.' Frantically Didier turned the page of his notepad and went on scribbling, not lifting his eyes from what he was writing.

For a moment the spell was broken. Anita looked from face to face, searching for something. Finally she asked for an ashtray. The psychiatrist found a kidney dish in a cupboard and she ground out her cigarette. 'Have you got another?' she asked almost immediately. Pel produced the packet and placed it on the bed; he flicked the lighter into action and waited.

'When we were behind the bushes he pushed me against the wall. I banged my head and wanted to cry out but I'd lost my voice. He was tearing at my clothes.' She inhaled deeply. Pel needed to stub out his cigarette, but he held it motionless between his fingers. 'He pulled off my anorak and threw it on the ground, then he ripped my skirt off and pushed me down. He smacked my face, that hurt!' She touched her cheek, then let her hand fall back on to the bed. 'He punched me a lot, then he pulled off my boots and tore my tights and knickers off. I knew what he was going to do and told myself I mustn't struggle. But I couldn't help it, I didn't want him to, he was hurting me, smacking, punching, trying to poke his thing into me. I didn't want him to.' She looked miserably at the policeman. 'I wanted to stop him, but he kept on smashing at me with his fist, then I saw the knife in his hand and I gave in.' She took a long drag at her cigarette. 'And he, he . . .' She dissolved in great sobbing tears, pulling her knees up and cradling them in her arms.

The psychiatrist moved towards her. 'Don't touch me!' she screamed. 'Keep away from me, doctor of madness! I want them to hear what I've got to say!' She stared wild-eyed at Pel and Annie and Didier. 'Catch the bastard that did it, catch him and I'll scratch the eyes from his face, I'll crush his balls, I'll cut it off for him and cook it and serve it to him for dinner. With chips!' She sobbed, dreadful wracking sobs that shook her whole body. Two nurses came into the room alerted by the shouting. The doctor whispered something to them and they turned and left, returning a moment later with a filled syringe sitting delicately in a small plastic tray.

Pel finally dropped his cigarette into the kidney dish and reached for another. The girl was desperately trying to regain control.

'Did you see his face?' he asked gently.

'That's all I see day and night.'

'Tell me.'

'I see darkness, then shadows, from the shadows a face emerges. I can't see it clearly but I have the impression of short dark hair with scarlet flashes. Please don't think I'm mad,' she said sadly, 'but this is what I see in my head, short dark hair, small blue eyes, cold blue, hooked nose, thin mean mouth in a beard, a short curly thick beard. I hate beards!' She fell back on the pillow exhausted while a nurse introduced the needle into her arm. She was quiet, all energy spent.

Didier Darras had efficiently noted the description but, as he expected, Debray was going to be sent to the hospital with his Porta-Portrait computer to get a proper picture. 'Tell him to get over there early tomorrow,' Pel said. 'The psychiatrist wouldn't let him near her today. Perhaps for once he's right.'

Darcy and Nosjean needed clarification, so they'd gone to see Cham in his pathology lab about his report on the death of Monsieur Bonnet, Roger. 'He was not killed by the blow to the head,' he said, 'although it was considerable. The point of impact was his temple, very sensitive, it could have killed him, but we found traces of sawdust in his nasal passages and floating in the blood in his lungs, which indicates he was still breathing but unconscious when the wood landed on top of him. From the marks on his chest, it was the logs that broke two of his ribs, one of which caused some internal bleeding, the other of which punctured a lung, hence the blood-filled lungs. In fact he drowned in his own blood. I had a devil of a job determining when he died. Rigor mortis was not present when his body was frozen for the first time, he thawed partially and was subsequently deep frozen afterwards. All this interferes considerably with my calculations, but I finally came up with the answer; he died during the night of the nineteenth of December. I'm sorry I can't be more precise.'

Darcy and Nosjean looked at each other – that was the date Claudine had last seen him.

'He died before his wife then, so he's not her murderer.'

'Could she have killed him?' Nosjean suggested.

'By ordering a mountain of logs to be dropped on him?' Cham asked, smiling.

'One thing at a time,' Darcy said. 'I think we'll be able to be more precise about the time of his death once we've seen the woodman.'

'What was he hit with?' Nosjean asked. 'Another log?'

Cham hung his head. 'Five tonnes of them, but the damage to his temple's got me completely foxed,' he said. 'I've tried every weapon on file, even the unlikely ones in desperation, but nothing fits. I honestly don't know.'

The telephone rang and Cham picked it up. After a moment he passed it to Darcy. 'It's for you,' he said.

'Monsieur Darcy, Daniel? Are you the next of kin to Madame Henri, Catherine?'

'Kate!'

He listened briefly and slammed the phone back down, running for the door.

13

With the light on the roof of the Range Rover flashing, Darcy took off like a bat out of hell. He had no siren but his hand never left the horn; he switched on the headlights and defied any *motard* to stop him for speeding. Leaving the doors open and the engine running he tore into Urgences, to be stopped dead by a nurse asking him if she could be of help.

'My wife,' he said, 'no, she's not my wife, my girlfriend, the woman I live with, she had an accident, where is she?'

Calmly the nurse asked for Monsieur's name and the name of his wife, girlfriend, or woman. Darcy couldn't remember. Panic was rising at a million miles an hour. 'Kate!' he said suddenly. 'Catherine Henri!'

'Ah yes, please follow me.'

They went through automatic doors and down miles of corridor, passing small cubicles with beds, lights and sometimes doctors and patients. They turned numerous corners into more miles of corridor until finally they stopped in a small room decorated with chairs and a low table covered with magazines.

'Please wait here,' the nurse told him and left.

Darcy paced round the table. He picked up a magazine and threw it down again. He sat, he stood, then he went on pacing. At long last the door to Radiology opened.

'So the X-rays show nothing?' he heard.

'Kate?'

She was upright, walking, talking, smiling, coming towards him.

'I thought you were dead!'

'Not yet,' she replied, kissing him, 'but the car is.'

Miraculously Kate was only bruised, her safety belt had saved her life. Her left shoulder was black and blue where she'd collided with the door as it hit the ground and she'd been told that for at least a week she'd feel like an old woman aching in places she hadn't known existed, but that was all.

'For crying out loud, Kate,' Darcy called from the kitchen, 'I thought you'd had it.'

'Well, I hadn't, but I'd really like to have that brandy you've been promising.'

Darcy needed the brandy more than Kate. 'Jesus, I was terrified.'

'So was I.'

'Kate, you've got to marry me. Next month, it only takes three weeks to do the necessary.'

'Quicker than buying a house.' She laughed. 'Look, we'll talk about that later, the boys are due back any minute. Right now I've got to think about supper.'

'The boys! What happened to them?'

'I climbed out of the wreck and walked to the school to collect them. I was slightly dazed but I felt okay. As the kids started streaming out of the classrooms the playground started whirling and I keeled over – delayed shock, I suppose. A friend called the ambulance and took the boys home. I guess when they came to collect the car they found my papers and called you.'

Towards midnight Kate woke from a nightmare. Darcy put his arms round her.

'It's over,' he said, 'you're all right. You're here at home, the boys are in bed, everything's all right.'

She whimpered into his neck and relaxed.

Three more times she woke that night, crying out, believing the boys had been in the back of the car and that she'd killed them.

'No,' Darcy soothed, 'they're in bed asleep. Don't worry, we're all here.'

'I was pushed,' she said sleepily.

Darcy stroked her hair, which fell like velvet across his chest. At last her body went limp and she fell into a deep slumber.

'She climbed out and limped away.' His voice was dull in the early hours of the morning. 'I watched from the hillside above. She's still around and probably telling tales.'

'Jesus, do I have to do everything myself? Okay, I'll sort her out, but you're coming with me for a lesson in how to deal with women.'

Nosjean didn't like leaving Mijo. Her back ached, her legs were swollen, her face was without make-up and looking tired. She waddled like a duck across the apartment to brew their breakfast coffee. Please let it happen soon, he prayed, please let me be there.

Darcy didn't like leaving Kate. He'd boiled the eggs for the boys, leaving her to sleep, now that she was finally able to. But she'd staggered down the old oak stairs to sip at her bowl of tea.

'God, I ache.'

'Bound to,' he said, 'but don't worry, it won't last long. A couple of days and you'll be fine.'

The boys looked anxiously at their mother. 'Don't worry,' he reassured them. 'When you come back this evening, she'll be almost back to normal.'

He was wrong, terribly wrong.

14

Darcy spent most of the morning tracking down the *bucheron* who had delivered the logs to the Bonnet house. He wasn't on the phone, so shortly after lunch he called to Nosjean and they set off to see him. The enormous shabby house was at the end of a bleak empty road; there wasn't a tree in sight, just an immense square of concrete in front of the building, decorated with neat stacks of cut wood. They came to a halt and looked about them. An old tractor and trailer sat in a makeshift hangar. Beside them was a Citroën car that looked anything but legal; everything was falling off it, the mudguards, the door handles, even the aerial had been replaced by a bent coat hanger. The house looked no better. A sharp wind whipped up from the fields below, tearing at their trouser legs as they crossed the yard to the front door. A dilapidated shutter banged open and they were confronted by a small, grey-haired woman demanding to know what they wanted. She was holding a rifle.

Both Darcy and Nosjean showed her their identification; the red, white and blue stripe was unfailingly recognisable even to those who couldn't read.

'What 'ave we done, then?' the woman demanded between broken black teeth.

'Nothing, madame,' Nosjean explained, 'but Monsieur Poux made a delivery of wood to Madame Bonnet on the nineteenth of December and we'd like to know what time he left the logs outside the house.' He was shivering and was anxious to get inside for a moment to warm himself up.

The gun disappeared with the old woman and shortly afterwards the front door opened on to a cheerless room. They went inside and waited while Madame Poux called her son. There was a vast fireplace but only a small fire burning in the grate, which was held up by half a dozen breeze blocks. There was a table and rough benches, a sideboard with a door missing, a sink and a single tap; the rest of the room was bare and stained brown. Both policemen installed themselves in front of the few flames to warm their backsides.

Eventually Monsieur Poux arrived. A wiry little man with a twinkle in his eye, he had the same set of teeth as his mother and although he looked undernourished, his biceps bulged out of a thin short-sleeved T-shirt like a couple of footballs. Darcy and Nosjean, both huddled in heavy overcoats, were still cold.

They sat round the table as the mother fetched a bottle and four dirty glasses. Having briefly wiped each one carefully on her filthy apron she placed them by the bottle and began pouring.

It looked like water, but having been caught out before, Darcy and Nosjean sipped gingerly at the liquid. For a moment neither of them could speak: it was pure fire.

As they left, Darcy couldn't help laughing. Nosjean was looking decidedly sick. 'The Poux are aptly named,' he said, 'and don't worry about the dirty glasses – that stuff was strong enough to kill all household germs.'

'Cleaning the lavatory is about all it's good for, how on earth did you manage to finish it?'

'I closed my eyes and thought of Chirac.'

'I take it back, that stuff is also good for making bombs. Well, at least we now know when Roger Bonnet died.'

'*Oui*, he arrived home around six and Poux delivered the logs about an hour later.'

'He must've been attacked almost immediately after his

wife slapped his face. A bit of time was needed for the snow to cover the body – Poux didn't see anything or anyone.'

'This time, we get it right, *d'accord*?'

'Should be a doddle, she's all on her own.'

'You sure there's no one else in there with her?'

'Only the dog. Christ! The bloody dog, he's as big as a bloody bull and ferocious as a bloody lion.'

'Now you tell me.'

'So what do we do?'

'We wait.'

They waited, the van well hidden in the woods, the two men hidden in the undergrowth and bushes opposite the house, sitting silently smoking and watching the front door. The only thing moving was the washing flapping lazily on the line to one side of the wood-shed. As they began swigging wine from a bottle they'd bought, the klaxon in the village three kilometres away announced midday. By one thirty the bottle was empty and they were ready for anything. Just before two o'clock the front door opened and a massive black dog charged out. He stopped dead, sniffing the air and enjoying the beginning of spring, then he cocked a leg at the wheel of an old van, scratched briefly in a patch of grass and trotted off down the lane.

They waited while Rasputin disappeared before they rose from their hiding place and headed quietly for the door.

In the city, Mijo cleared away her plate, knife and fork. She was fed up and bored with carrying ten extra kilos. Every night she went to bed hoping it might just wake her up, every morning she laboriously rose and prayed it would be today. But nothing happened, she was still pregnant and beginning to resent it. Everything was ready, the clothes, the cot; her bags were packed with tiny pyjamas, vests, booties and disposable nappies. Nothing had been forgotten, they'd been through it a million times. Nosjean left numerous telephone numbers so she could reach him and still he rang her often, just in case. But nothing happened, so she waited, heavy and unhappy.

When the phone rang she expected it to be her husband but to her surprise it was Kate.

'Oh come on,' she said finally, 'an afternoon in the country will do you good. You can't sit cogitating forever, the baby'll arrive when she's ready. We'll take the dog out for a gallop through the woods, it'll do you good. I'll regale you with tales of childbirth and tell you how ghastly it all is!'

Laughing, Mijo agreed to spend a peaceful afternoon in the countryside with Kate. They'd only met once but policemen's wives had few friends and with the feeling that Kate might just become one she called a taxi and locked the door, leaving the baby paraphernalia behind her.

When the car drew away from the end of the lane she started walking towards the house. For the first time in months she felt free, breathing in the pale sunshine, smelling the earth and the trees, the cold wind freshening her face. She smiled. Dear Kate, thank you for ringing, an afternoon in the country was just what she needed.

As she approached the house she called out. The washing was sulking on the line, an old van was dumped inelegantly in the corner – she'd heard about the crash and supposed the van was a temporary replacement. It all looked peaceful and normal but the more she called the more she felt something was missing. There was no reply, but that wasn't it. There was nothing, no noise at all, just the trees whispering to one another. She noticed with surprise that one of the large front windows was broken, demolished, wood and glass alike smashed into an enormous hole. The front door was wide open and hesitantly she stepped inside, calling for Kate. Momentarily she stared unbelieving.

As her head started swimming, the nausea rose from the

pit of her stomach. She grabbed the door and forced herself to concentrate; finally regaining her balance she went unsteadily across the room to the phone.

Help was on its way. Mijo wondered what to do. She knew she was incapable of helping Kate – every time she looked at her bloody body, her stomach churned, her head swam. She had to get out, breathe fresh air, wait for the ambulance. The dog had been hidden behind an upturned table; as Mijo made her way to the door, she saw him and bent over to see if he was dead. The sharp pain caught her by surprise, it was like a fire igniting at the base of her spine. She cried out, clutching at her sides, turning to see who had hurt her, but what she saw was her own blood oozing on to the floor, a large red puddle forming at her feet. Darkness swirled up, smothering her strength and stealing the pain away; she slipped into the black hole of unconsciousness.

15

Pel wondered how he was going to tell them. It was bad enough when it was someone you didn't know, but he was going to have to confront Darcy and Nosjean, he knew them both well, and now the time had come to consider it, he damn well liked them. Unlike a lot of men they adored their wives – how the hell was he going to tell them? The ashtray was overflowing and his lungs felt as if they were full of cinders. There was only one way. He frowned as he replaced the phone; no one knew where they were. Slamming out of his office and making the window panes rattle, he headed for the sergeants' room where he found Pujol and Rigal in residence.

'Where are Darcy and Nosjean?' he shouted.

'Sir, I'm sorry, but, well, they went out half an hour ago and – '

'Where?'

'They didn't say.'

'Find them!'

Back in his office he rang Pomereu, head of Traffic. 'Don't ask any questions,' he ordered, 'but I want you to find a Range Rover, dark green, *immatriculation* number 1574 RB 21. I want it doing now! When you find it tell the occupants, Inspectors Darcy and Nosjean, to contact me immediately. No slip-ups. I want them within the next half-hour!' He smashed the phone back down and went storming to the sergeants' room.

'Well?'

'No luck yet, sir.'

'Try harder! Contact everyone, find out where they are, they must be found, now.'

Darcy and Nosjean were sitting comfortably in the offices of Leisure Pleasure interviewing a very embarrassed Jacques Barthes and his secretary. They'd walked in unannounced and found them gaily making love behind a filing cabinet. They were denying it but that's certainly what it had looked like. Having allowed them a moment to readjust their clothes, they were now sipping coffee and smothering grins. Both Barthes and the young woman were pink in the face and smothering their embarrassment.

While they were at an advantage, Darcy dropped his bombshell about Barthes' car being seen outside the Bonnet house the night Claudine died. He looked surprised, then smugly commented that only a fool would have taken a car out in that snow.

That was all they needed, no one had mentioned the snow. Sulkily, both Barthes and his secretary agreed to go the Hôtel de Police and make a statement.

They were put into separate interview rooms when they arrived at the Hôtel de Police. Annie Saxe sat with the secretary while Bardolle guarded Barthes; neither of them was saying anything. As Darcy and Nosjean decided on the line of attack they should take Pujol finally found them.

'The Patron wants to see you both urgently,' he said.

'We had a couple of traffic cops from Police Municipale tell us the same thing but he'll have to wait, we've got a couple of important clients to see to.'

'I don't think he'll wait, he's been shouting ever since you left.'

Darcy looked at Nosjean, who shrugged. 'I suppose we could always let them sweat for a bit.'

Pel was sitting with his head in his hands, a cigarette

smouldering in the ashtray. He looked up as they came through the door, allowing his specs to slip back into place. Pel rubbed his face and stubbed out his half-smoked cigarette. Darcy noticed: something was wrong, seriously wrong. The Patron never extinguished a Gauloise before sucking the very last lungful from it.

Pel removed his glasses searching for the words as both men drew up chairs and sat.

'I don't know what happened,' Pel started, 'I mean, you'll have to ask Cheriff when he gets back with Aimedieu, they were the ones who went to see ...' His voice trailed off. Neither man had ever seen Pel lost for words. Darcy raised an eyebrow. 'It was after they got there Cheriff called in and told me ... Holy Mother of God!' he shouted banging his fist on the desk. 'Get down to the hospital, it's Kate and Mijo.'

As the Hôtel de Police prepared to pack up for the evening Pujol insinuated himself round Pel's door.

'Yes?' he hissed.

Pujol took two paces back. 'Annie and Bardolle want to know what they're supposed to do with Monsieur Barthes and his secretary.'

'They can do what they like with them, as far as I'm concerned,' Pel replied without looking up.

'Should they release them? They've been waiting to be interviewed for over two hours now.'

'Interviewed? What the hell are you on about?'

'Darcy and Nosjean brought them in, but I can't find them anywhere and Monsieur Barthes is becoming impatient. The secretary's started crying.'

Pel lit up, took a deep breath and stared at Pujol. 'Do you know why they were brought in?'

'No, sir. They are investigating Claudine Bonnet's murder and went out shortly after lunch. When they came back – '

'Have Barthes and his secretary been arrested?'

'No, sir, just brought in to make a statement, something to

111

do with them having an affair and Barthes knowing about the weather the night Madame Bonnet died. I heard that much as I came along the corridor to tell them you wanted – '

'You know more than you think. Get me the file on Claudine Bonnet and meet me outside the interview rooms five minutes ago.'

'Sir!'

'And Pujol, as you seem to know something you'd better swot up on the contents of the file as you're walking down the corridor so you know a lot more by the time you arrive,' he smiled and succeeded in terrifying Pujol, 'because you'll be interviewing the secretary.'

While Pel had a go at Barthes, pretending he knew exactly what he was after, Pujol meticulously and kindly asked the secretary for answers to anything he thought might be relevant and a lot else besides.

When the two men at last came back into the corridor Pel looked at Pujol the Puppy.

'Well?'

'Well, she was apparently having a bit of an affair with both her bosses, although neither knew about the other, which is why she has denied it all along.'

'And Claudine Bonnet?'

'She'd only ever met her once, at a Christmas dinner a few years ago, and didn't like her very much. She's never seen her since although she feels she knows her quite well from what her husband told her. But as she said, she was having an affair with the husband and it is very likely that he exaggerated to gain her sympathy and her, well, you know.'

'No, I don't know, spit it out, man. To gain her sympathy and her what?'

'Her body,' Pujol replied, staring at his shoes.

'Is she telling the truth?'

'I think so, but I have very little experience in judging these matters.'

'Agreed. What do you suggest we do with her now?'

Pujol look surprised and desperately anxious. 'Release her, sir?'

'Correct,' Pel said. 'Do it, then come into my office. We've got work to do.'

'And Monsieur Barthes?'

'Already released.'

As Pel and Pujol pondered over the Bonnet file with the two statements they'd taken, Darcy and Nosjean sat by their wives' beds. Mijo was conscious but sleeping. Kate had just come back from the operating theatre where they'd put a dozen stitches in her hands and another dozen under her chin. They'd also reattached the underneath of her left breast. A tube ran from an apparatus into her left arm delivering blood to replace what she'd lost. Into her right arm was another drip, he didn't know what that was. But at least the doctors were no longer shaking their heads, they weren't saying much at all. Darcy watched her silent white face, her closed eyes, those beautiful eyes that had smiled and promised wicked things they'd enjoyed together, and her body so lifeless, a body that usually bounced and leapt with fun, a body he loved and lusted after always. He nearly wept.

Annie came out of the interview room tired; what she wanted was a long hot bath and an equally long cold beer. All she had to do was collect her things from the sergeants' room and escape across the city to her flat. Then she remembered Brigitte Breille – she'd promised to drop in and make sure she was all right. Damn, the bath and the beer would have to wait. But they were going to have to wait longer than she thought.

When she went into the sergeants' room she found Cheriff playing with two small boys. 'Starting a *garderie*?' she asked, idly plucking her coat off the peg.

'Nope, these are Kate's kids, James and Edward.'

The two boys politely shook hands.

'What are they doing here? Is Mum coming to get you?'

'Our mother has had a bit of an accident.'

'But that was yesterday,' Annie said, puzzled.

'She's had another.'

Cheriff tousled the hair of the larger boy, and signalled to Annie to follow him. He closed the door behind them as they stepped into the corridor.

'I was called out to an attempted murder,' he said quietly. 'It was Kate.'

'Oh, God, no!'

'Darcy's at the hospital waiting but he rang to ask someone to collect the boys from school. I can't take them home, the lab boys are still at the house. What the hell am I supposed to do with them? By the way, Nosjean's at the hospital too – it looks as if Mijo surprised the intruder.'

'Oh, shit. Is Pel still around?'

'Yes, and busy.'

'Look, how about taking them to the hospital in a marked police car – they'll enjoy that.'

'I don't think they should see their mother.'

'That bad? But they can see Darcy, he'll tell us what to do.'

Darcy was looking exhausted when he came into the waiting-room. The sparkle had gone from his eyes and the Disney smile had disappeared. He hugged the boys, blinking hard.

'Thanks,' he said simply to Annie and Cheriff. 'I needed that.'

'What are we going to do with the little blighters?' Cheriff asked cheerfully. 'They can't stay here all night.'

'They need to go home,' Darcy said.

'For the moment that won't be possible.'

Darcy nodded understanding. 'Then I don't know. I don't want to leave Kate yet. Look,' he said taking out his wallet, 'how about treating them to McDonald's? I'll phone home

114

and tell them to get a move on. By the time you've finished eating, the coast should be clear. I'll come back as soon as I can.'

He hugged the now bouncing boys, telling them to be good, and turned back towards the ward. 'Take care of them,' he added, 'they're precious.'

16

The following morning Pel was ready to fire the entire police force. The morning meeting was short and deadly; his team was pleased to escape to tramp the streets in a biting wind. No one wanted to be anywhere near him.

'Darcy, Nosjean, you wait,' he ordered, watching them both turn to go. 'The Chief wants a word.'

The Chief squeezed his way through the door and offered his regret for what had happened.

'Tell me about it,' he said.

For once Darcy was looking like Prince Charming who'd had a hard night. Pel had always longed to see it but now he hoped it wasn't permanent. 'There's not a lot to tell. As far as I could make out nothing was stolen,' Darcy said slowly. 'A lot was broken but not missing. Kate was in no fit state to talk last night although she did open her eyes. From the look of our house there was a fight, someone attacked her with a knife, she defended herself, hence the cuts on her hands and,' he paused to light a cigarette, 'and elsewhere. There must have been quite a lot of noise, probably Kate screaming – Rasputin leapt through the window, God knows why, maybe he saw her attacker from outside and went the fastest way in, maybe they'd locked the door.'

'Rasputin?'

'The dog, he's a Beauceron, a gentle giant, but no one lays a finger on Kate or the kids while he's around. He must have been outside taking a leak when ... anyway, they shot him.' Darcy sighed. 'He's gone off to the vet's but I don't think he'll live. However, they did find a piece of cloth and what looked like a lump of meat in his mouth. I've had it sent to the lab in the hope it might have been part of the attacker. If it was it'll explain why they didn't finish Kate off completely.'

'How is she?'

'Weak but alive.'

'That's something,' the Chief said, turning to Nosjean who stood with his hands in his pockets, a cigarette hanging limply from his lips. 'Tell me the rest.'

Nosjean removed the cigarette. 'Kate'd rung Mijo and invited her over for the afternoon. When she got there she discovered Kate, unconscious and covered in blood. She telephoned for an ambulance, then she came across the dog – he was behind an upturned table. She bent down to see if he was asleep or dead and in doing so provoked a massive haemorrhage. The baby's due any day now.'

'So she wasn't attacked?'

'No. They found no wounds on her, just a lot of blood on the floor. It was the baby.'

'She lost it?'

'No. They thought it was likely but last night they did an *échographie* and it's okay. Except,' he added, 'it's breech and they're talking about a Caesarean section birth.'

'Translate,' Pel said. 'You lost me there.'

'It doesn't matter, Patron, there's a good chance both of them'll be all right.'

'Fine. We'll have to wait for Forensics to finish their report before we can make any headway – that, and Kate will have to be properly questioned when she's ready. In the meantime, let's get back to the Bonnet murder.' Pel opened the file. 'You brought his partner and the secretary in yesterday. Pujol and I interviewed them. The secretary is a bit of a loose woman but I believe so far has nothing to do with the death of Claudine Bonnet. Barthes, on the other hand, I'm not sure about. He told me Claudine rang the evening she died, his wife took the call and passed it over to Barthes. Claudine said she was worried about the business with her husband missing, his body hadn't been found yet if you remember, and she would like to talk to Barthes. He resisted, it was snowing already and he didn't fancy spending an evening with a depressed woman. She's been depressed for some time and he thinks she may have been drinking. We now know she was an alcoholic, so far it rings true. So he was wary of going to talk to her. But she insisted, implored him to go over.' Pel removed his glasses briefly and looked up. 'Was this a game they played to hide an affair they were having? Barthes liked the ladies.'

'That's doubtful,' Darcy said. 'The autopsy report showed she hadn't had sex for a long time.'

Pel reluctantly had to agree and replacing his glasses he went on. 'He says that finally he gave in and drove to the house. At the crossroads the snow had already drifted and he didn't want to risk going down the slip road in front of the house so he parked the car at the side of the main road. He got out of the car and was about to leg it to the garden gate when he happened to look up at the bedroom window. Something had caught his eye, he said. The light was on up there and he could clearly see Claudine getting dressed. She was parading back and forth, discarding one dress to try another. He watched horrified, realising she was getting ready for him. He says it was obvious she was tarting herself up and he wanted none of it.'

Pel wearily reached out for his packet of cigarettes. 'I still wonder if they'd had an affair some time ago and Barthes had rejected her. Without her husband she was trying to get him back and becoming a nuisance.'

'That's possible, but could he have seen her so clearly through the falling snow?' the Chief asked. 'It was snowing heavily that evening.'

'He could have seen enough. The next-door neighbour, Madame Richard, saw him standing by the car. Anyway, he decided not to stay and got back in the car to leave, but he was stuck. At this point he started to panic. The noise of him revving the car might draw her attention in which case he wouldn't be able to escape. At last the next-door neighbour, Guy Richard – we've seen him and he confirms this part of the story – came to his rescue with a shovel and helped him out of his predicament. He went home, told his wife he couldn't get through and settled down in front of the television.'

'What time did Madame Richard see him standing by the car?'

'She thinks between nine and half-past, that's the children's bedtime, she saw him having switched their lights off.'

'And what time did her husband go out to help him?'

'About half an hour later, the children were misbehaving and he went to shut them up. They have a window on their landing and going past it he noticed someone stuck at the crossroads.'

'So Barthes easily had the time to go to the house and kill Claudine Bonnet.'

'He had the time to have a drink with her and start the meal she'd prepared, then kill her.'

'Why did he disappear for a couple of days afterwards?'

'He says he had a row with his wife and decided to teach her a lesson. He went to Paris with his secretary to a swimming pool exhibition.'

'In January?'

'Odd, but it's true. It's at the Halle d'Exposition in Neuilly, we checked.'

'What was the row about?'

'She has a lover, he says, and he doesn't like it.'

'But he was carrying on with the secretary.'

'That's not our problem. We've got to see his wife and find out what she's got to offer. Then we'll bring him in again.'

'Arrest him?' the Chief asked hopefully.

'No, we can't yet, there's not enough evidence, but we may be able to persuade him to confess, if we're crafty. You might trip him up into giving us a clue on Roger Bonnet's death – he could have been responsible for both. We'd better inter-view Barthes' wife, she may be able to throw some light on the subject of her husband's behaviour that night. Darcy and Nosjean, get on with it,' Pel said. 'You can call at the hospital on your way back.'

Annie knocked and came in. 'Patron, excuse me for interrupting, but it may be important. Last night at Darcy's and Kate's house, Cheriff was getting the boys upstairs and into bed as fast as possible, while I did a bit of clearing up downstairs, it was a mess.' Pel was wondering what Cheriff was doing putting boys to bed but he let it pass. 'While I was sweeping I found this.' She placed a small gold circle on the desk. It was broken at one side and slightly bent. 'It's an earring,' she explained.

Darcy looked at it. 'Kate never wears hoops in her ears, she says it makes her look like a gypsy, and she's the only woman in the house.'

'Blokes wear ear-rings nowadays,' Annie pointed out. 'Kate may have wrenched it from her attacker's ear while she fought him off.'

'Well, it's not a lot but it's something. Thank you, Annie. We're now looking for a man with a sore ear and possibly a large hole in his arse. If the lab confirms that what they found in the dog's mouth was human flesh, find out what part of the body it actually came from and alert the hospitals.'

Darcy and Nosjean were received by Jacques Barthes' robust wife, who quite delightedly told them she knew all about her husband's affair with the secretary and wasn't in the least bit surprised that Roger Bonnet was accused of doing the same thing. Her opinion was that everyone was at it, including herself; at least it helped avoid boredom in an established marriage. She confirmed that he had set off in the snow to see Claudine Bonnet but had come home cross and cold, claiming to have got stuck in a drift. Laughing, she pointed out that her husband often came home cold and cross but that night his trouser legs were wet to the knees. He'd changed and fallen asleep in front of the television while she slipped off to bed alone for a good night's sleep. Darcy wondered who inherited the Bonnet half of the firm now both of them were dead. Madame Barthes wondered why the hell she hadn't thought of it sooner but was unable to say who inherited what. She did however give them the name and address of the firm's solicitor and waved them off, cheerfully asking them to let her know if she'd become a wealthy woman.

Darcy and Nosjean in particular found the whole episode rather depressing.

'But at least she told us the truth, that was obvious,' Darcy pointed out.

'About what?' Nosjean said, gloomily putting the car into gear and heading towards Centre Ville and the solicitor's office.

After they'd seen him they set off for the hospital. Darcy asked Nosjean what he thought.

'I think I'm leaving the police,' he replied.

Darcy pulled into the side of the road and switched off the engine. 'Why?'

Nosjean dragged a packet of cigarettes out of his pocket. 'This is why,' he said, offering them to Darcy. 'My nerves are in tatters, my wife's in hospital, my daughter was in danger of dying before she'd been born, and', he added, 'I'm smoking more than ever.'

'Come on, I'll buy you a drink.'

'Look,' Darcy said from behind his beer, 'don't just chuck it all up because of a few little hitches.'

'Little hitches!'

'Yes, I know, and I understand how you feel. Do you think the idea didn't cross my mind while I was sitting beside Kate waiting for her to come round and praying she'd be all right? When I got home and went to kiss the boys goodnight, they were asleep – they looked so innocent, so small, so vulnerable. Someone's got to protect the innocent and catch the criminals. You and I are good at it. It's the best thing we can do, keep at it, we have to be strong for them. Now, drink up and tell me what you think about the Bonnet case, that's what I asked you originally, you know.'

'I know, it's just that I've got so much on my mind, what with a wife, a baby, soon I expect it'll be a mortgage. Mijo being in danger just did for me. However,' he sighed, gulping at his glass, 'the solicitor repeated what Barthes said. The final clause of the Leisure Pleasure contract between the partners was put in on the solicitor's insistence in case of a car accident or something.'

'Something like murder.'

'No one was thinking of murder at the time, were they? Both partners thought it was ridiculous but finally agreed to tie up the legal end of things, saying if it didn't cost them any more he could add it on, it would never be put into force so it didn't count.'

'But now it has come into force and counts considerably. When they first started up they were two blokes with a dream of success. It happened and now they are both quite wealthy men.'

'Barthes is very wealthy now, and his jolly wife – they don't have to share any more, they've got the lot,' Nosjean pointed out.

'Supposing he did for Roger Bonnet to gain his part of Leisure Pleasure or out of jealousy for the secretary, perhaps he did know about them, then had to deal with Claudine because she was becoming a nuisance?'

'It was all very premeditated, but what I don't understand', Nosjean said, 'is how he managed to clobber Roger and shove him under a pile of logs.'

'The logs were luck, he could have counted on just the snow to hide him. It was snowing then too. Bonnet had snow still frozen on to his clothes under the logs; it was encrusted with wood dust, so the snow fell on him before the wood. Suppose Barthes left the office before Bonnet and waited for him to arrive; unfortunately the secretary took him home and his wife met him on the garden path, so his plans were foiled, until his wife slapped him and ran into the house. That was his chance, he called Bonnet to the gate and clobbered him one.'

'But it was a hell of a risk to take, he doesn't seem like the sort of man that would take risks like that. Why on earth would he leave him outside his garden gate?'

'Panic? Perhaps he was surprised by the tractor at the crossroads turning into the slip road in front of the house, so he scarpered, coming back later to move the body and discovering five tonnes of logs on top of it.'

'It's possible,' Nosjean agreed thoughtfully, 'but it's all perhaps. Somehow we've got to prove it. So far we've got nothing that would stand up in court.'

'Oh damn it,' Darcy concluded, 'let's go and see the ladies.'

Nosjean hesitated before climbing into the car. 'Don't mention what I said to anyone, will you? I haven't reached a decision yet.'

'Tell anyone what? As far as I can remember this conversation was about the Bonnet murders.'

'What do you mean she's still alive?'

'Look at the paper.' He handed it over to the tall man lying on his stomach.

'I don't believe it, and me like this. I can't even go and finish her off.'

'At least you got the dog.'

'Dogs can't talk.'

'And she got a good look at you.'

'She wasn't seeing anything by that time. It gives no description in the paper. Ring the police and find out what they really know.'

'What!'

'You heard me.'

'You go, she saw you not me.'

'*Espèce de con*, you know damn well I can't get up, I've got half my arse missing. Every time I get up I'm in fear of bleeding to death.'

17

Mijo was calm but looking worried. She'd been told by the doctors that all would be well, but when Nosjean arrived she burst into tears and was not to be consoled. He tried changing the subject and talking about what had happened to Kate in the hope she would remember some small detail that would help them, but she was incapable of discussing it and accused her husband of not caring about her or their unborn baby. It was not an easy hour.

Kate was calm; the drips had been removed from her arms and she was sitting propped up against a lot of pillows. As Darcy came through the door she was frowning while she scribbled with bandaged hands on a piece of paper.

'Hello, gorgeous,' he said, smiling.

'Come here and give us a kiss,' she replied, dropping the pencil on the bed. Unfortunately, more than a light peck on the cheek hurt like hell and eventually they gave up. Kate rested back on her pillows breathing heavily.

'God, it hurts,' she whispered, tears trickling out of her eyes. 'You wait till I'm recovered, we're going to have to make up for lost time.' She smiled weakly and allowed Darcy to brush the tears from her cheeks. 'How are the boys?'

'Leaping about and uncontrollable. Cheriff and Annie have been terrific. They looked after them last night and had them taken to school in a police car with the sirens blasting this morning. They'll be unbearable for years.'

'Take care of them, Darcy, they're all I've got.'

'You've got me,' he replied quietly. 'When are you going to let me make an honest woman of you?'

'As soon as I can defend myself we'll talk about it,' she said, 'but in the meantime I've been making a few notes. It's difficult to remember exactly, but if you're interested I'll try and tell you.'

Darcy sat on the end of the bed and listened.

'I let Rasputin out for a pee after lunch,' she started. 'While he was gone I rang Mijo and asked her over for the afternoon, but of course I never saw her – I hope you explained.'

'I told you last night but you won't remember. She found you, phoned for the ambulance and passed out. She's here in the hospital in Maternity, still waiting.'

'Poor Mijo, that must have been quite a shock. By the way, did Rasputin come home? The silly sod had wandered off, just when I needed him the most.'

Darcy swallowed hard, this wasn't going to be easy. 'He's at the vet's. He did come back, just in time.'

'Good old Rasputin, I hope he made mincemeat out of them.'

'Them?'

'There were two of them. Hey, why's Rasputin at the vet's? What happened to him?'

'They shot him. Did you get a look at them?'

'Yes and no. Will he be all right?'

'The vet's not over-confident. Can you describe them? Kate, are you okay?'

Kate's eyes were closed but seeping tears. 'No, I'm not, I'm sick to the stomach and seeking revenge. The bastards – get them, Darcy, you've got to get them. Rasputin was my best friend.' Abruptly, her eyes opened and she sat up wincing. 'I'd finished phoning Mijo and was washing up when I heard the door being opened. I turned round and saw two men standing just inside. They were both wearing cagoules, I could barely see their eyes let alone the rest of their faces. Jesus, I was frightened, but I managed to ask them what they wanted. The taller one replied, "You, Madame Darcy." He

126

was laughing. He produced a flick-knife and came for me round the side of the table. I'd already grabbed a kitchen knife under the water, I was still standing at the sink, remember, so I took it out and placed it on the draining-board, then I picked up a couple of glasses and hurled them at the smaller man – he was holding a small hunting rifle, it looked like a 12 mm. He dropped the gun so I hurled some more, plates too, anything I could lay my hands on.' She grinned. 'We're going to have to buy a lot of crockery, you know – I must have smashed most of it.'

'That doesn't matter, go on.'

'The little one, still by the door, ducked under the table, I suppose to retrieve the gun, but the other one, the one with the knife, kept coming for me. I had nothing left to throw so I picked up my kitchen knife and made like I knew how to handle it. He thought it was hilarious, so I slashed at him but all I did was scratch his leather jacket. He cut my outstretched hands so I tried to do the same. He started shouting, I started screaming. He grabbed me and was trying to remove my jumper, he didn't manage it but he almost removed my boob. That was awful. It's weird but it almost hurts more now thinking about it than when it actually happened – all the same it felt like he was setting me on fire. I lost the knife, but I kicked and punched, the trouble was he cut my hands too. We fell over in the struggle and then I felt the most dreadful burning by my ear and under my chin, then I guess I passed out. Although I do seem to remember a terrific smashing noise, a bit like an explosion and falling glass.'

'Rasputin, he came through the window. Kate, you realise this man was cutting your throat, don't you? If it hadn't been for Rasputin they'd have killed you. As it was they fled.'

'Not before shooting poor Ras.'

'You won't like me for this,' Darcy said quietly, 'but I'd rather lose him than you. So would the boys.'

She nodded sadly but continued. 'One was lightly built and probably smaller than me, but not much. He was wearing jeans, dirty white basketball boots, black leather jacket and woollen gloves, I think. His eyes were brown and ordinary, not large, small, squinting and so on.' She referred to her notes. 'The other was tall, about like you, well built, a bit like an athlete, but not a wrestler, if you know what I mean. He was wearing exactly the same except he had leather gloves with zips on them, they hurt.' She touched her swollen cheek. 'He seemed to enjoy what he was doing. His eyes were a very pale blue and he had blondish hair, short but touching his ears. He was clean-shaven.'

Darcy looked surprised. 'I thought they were wearing hoods?'

'They were, but I pulled one off, it was hanging round his neck when he bent over to cut my throat . . . oh God, Darcy.' The tears were tumbling out of her eyes again. Darcy went to her and as he gently put an arm round her shoulders she leant her head against him, exhausted.

'Would you recognise him again?' he asked gently.

'Yes.'

'I'll send Debray up with his portable computer.'

Debray took Annie to the hospital. She wanted to see Anita Tabeyse, the second rape victim, who was due to go home the following morning.

When they arrived at the hospital Debray headed straight for Kate's room while Annie went in the opposite direction down the same corridor. As Annie went in Anita was putting the finishing touches to her make-up. She was looking different, the swelling on her face had gone down and the stitches had been removed although the patchwork round her mouth was still very evident. She managed a smile and put down the mirror and mascara. 'What do you think?' she asked.

'It's good to see you looking almost normal again.'

'Thank you, I feel better. I'm trying to get into practice for tomorrow. I'm going home.'

'I know, that's why I'm here. We got a message that you'd

like to see a detective dealing with your case. Everyone's tied up this afternoon, so it's got to be me.'

'That's fine, I'd rather it was you. Look, Annie, it's something I remembered, probably insignificant, but Monsieur Pel said every little bit helps. He was wearing a gold ear-ring.'

'Who – Monsieur Pel?' Annie asked, laughing.

'No, you idiot, the man who attacked me.'

Annie wasn't laughing any more. 'You're sure?'

'Absolutely.'

Annie considered the information a moment, then made her decision. 'Would you fancy taking a stroll down the corridor to see another possible victim?'

'If she's as crazy as I was when I first came round, no, thank you.'

'She was badly cut, but she wasn't raped.'

'Then I don't see the connection. What do you want me to do?'

'Tell her what you just told me and I'll watch her reaction.'

Debray punched Kate's description into his Porta-Portrait computer but she shook her head. 'No, he had lighter coloured hair,' she said, closing her eyes and trying to conjure up in her head the face that had been indelibly printed on her brain a few hours earlier. It wasn't as easy as she'd expected, the details escaped her, but after a few false starts they were making progress. It was a sophisticated operation; the bad sketches had disappeared years ago, and the computer now provided photographs of details of millions of faces, knitting them together into a recognisable portrait. The result was a thousand times better than the artist's impression of the old days. Kate studied the face on the screen. 'He was better looking than that. Although his eyes were narrower, they were larger, set further apart.' Debray punched a few buttons and the face changed subtly.

Kate considered. 'His mouth was slightly wider. Mm, that's about it, but can you make him laugh?' She wasn't satisfied.

Annie knocked and came in with Anita. When the introductions were over Debray showed them the portrait he'd been working on with Kate.

'Not bad,' she said, 'but if that's my rapist you need to add a beard and put a small hoop ear-ring in one of his ears.'

Debray obliged with the ear-ring and a grim smile.

'My God,' Kate said quietly, 'that's him.'

He added a beard, left the smile and put the face in heavy shadow, turning his hair dark. It made Anita tremble when she saw the result. She was sure.

'Well, at least we know what he looks like,' Debray said to Annie. 'Now we've got to put a name to him and find out where he is.'

Within hours the portrait was faxed to television stations and the newspapers. They wanted full coverage and most of all they wanted him found. They still had no name, they still didn't know who the second man was.

A second man had entered Kate's life and she was enjoying his company. Cheriff had collected her two sons and had delivered them to her hospital room. They flung themselves at her, unaware of the agony they were causing; hugs and kisses were exchanged and a lot of chattering went on. He'd brought a picnic tea for them and while they leapt round the room scattering crumbs, Cheriff sat unperturbed, cutting pieces of bread and dealing biscuits.

'You look as if you've been doing that all your life,' Kate said.

'I'm the oldest of seven children,' he explained. 'My father left us when I was twelve, so it's habit.'

'Thank you for looking after them last night.'

'It was the least we could do, and I did have some help. Annie's great – for once she didn't break anything.'

'There wasn't much left to break, was there?' She laughed.

'Not much,' Cheriff replied, laughing back.

'How's Darcy coping?' she asked.

'He's coping fine,' he said, standing in the doorway and wearing a scowl that would have looked good on Pel. 'You can leave now,' he added coldly.

'Do you need me at the house this evening?'

'No, go to your own home.'

'Call me if you need me.'

The boys didn't want Cheriff to leave, but promising he'd see them the following day he said goodnight and Darcy closed the door firmly behind him. He was seething with an emotion he'd never felt before and it showed on his taut good-looking face.

18

Misset had drunk enough tea for a lifetime. Nini was very sweet, like the tea, but totally uninterested in anything more than brewing up and gossiping. The cushy number he thought he'd pulled had turned out to be plain boring. He'd listened dozens of times to her description of the men who worked on the *zone industrielle*. He knew one of them wore pink socks occasionally – so what? Big deal. In an effort to ingratiate himself and to help their friendship along, he'd sported a pink tie one morning. She was ecstatic, for five minutes. He decided she was completely loopy. Her whole house was decorated from top to bottom in various shades of pink, she dressed day after day in a collection of pink dungarees. Behind her house she even had a small pink swimming pool. It seemed crazy; on the edge of an industrial estate here was a small piece of pink paradise and it wasn't turning Misset on a bit. He wanted to give up. He'd ask Pel to find him something else to do, tramping round the bars looking for someone perhaps, that would fit the bill. He liked showing off his badge in bars, it impressed the girls, trouble was there were fewer and fewer girls in the bars – the good girls stayed out of them and the bad girls didn't stay long. Perhaps he'd have another go with the Pink. She was quite pretty really, although rather too round. She was divorced, her two children were well behaved and went to bed early, but all that tea – he was drowning by the end of the day. It was no good asking Pel for a transfer, he knew it, he'd get himself shouted at or fired.

When Misset came in that evening there were only Pujol

and Rigal in the sergeants' room. The phone was ringing so he pulled rank and, perching himself inelegantly on the edge of the desk, answered it, thinking that when he'd finished perhaps he could boss them about a bit.

'Sergeant Misset *à l'appareil*,' he said importantly.

'Good evening. I'm ringing about Madame Darcy – how is she?'

'Just one moment, I'll find out.' He turned to Pujol for information.

'Oh, good,' the caller said when he'd been told she was recovering. 'And the man who attacked her, have you any leads?'

'Just a minute.' Misset again turned to Pujol, who hesitated before shaking his head. He closed the file in front of him and headed for the door.

'No,' Misset replied, 'no leads so far.'

'Are you sure? What are you doing about it? Surely you must know something?'

Misset wasn't prepared to admit that he hadn't the foggiest idea but with a flash of brilliance, he thought, he announced that all information on the leads they had was, of course, confidential.

'And Monsieur Darcy, how's he?'

'Same as usual. Don't you worry,' he added smugly, 'we're on to them.'

'Thank you, thank you very much.'

Misset replaced the receiver, pleased with himself.

Pel was staring at another report. The lab had just confirmed that the piece of meat the vet had removed from Rasputin's mouth was part of a human being's backside, the human being that had tried to slit Kate's throat, the human being that had raped Anita Tabeyse and Brigitte Breille – it was the same blood group. Perhaps they were dealing with a maniac. Thinking about the consequences, Pel was already in a bad mood before Pujol knocked at his door.

'It's late and I'm busy,' he snarled, 'so don't start bothering me with your cock problems.'

'No, sir, I think I can sort that one out. I've been studying the by-laws and the *droits de passage* on the farmland and I'm sure we can find a solution. But it wasn't that, it was something else, something silly that you'll probably shout at me for.'

'Me? Shout?' Pel looked startled.

'I'll take the risk just in case it's important.'

Pel was slowly beginning to discover that Pujol had hidden depths. 'Well, *accouche*,' he said sharply, petrifying Pujol.

'A call has just come through about Madame Darcy – they wanted to know how she was and whether we have any leads.'

'You took the call?'

'No, sir, Sergeant Misset.'

'Oh, God, tell me what he said.'

'Well, he referred to me. At first I wasn't quick enough and confirmed that Madame Darcy was recovering. Then when he asked about leads I shook my head and left the room.'

'So you don't know what Misset said?'

'Yes, I do, I listened from the switchboard. He told the caller there were no leads as yet but that we were on to them.'

'So?'

'Madame has had two attempts on her life already.'

'What makes you say that?'

'I've been going through the files, genning up so to speak, and I wondered if her car accident was really an accident or whether she was deliberately pushed. At the end of the statement Darcy brought in she says she thought there may have been another vehicle, certainly when I went to see her car it looked as if something had collided with her back wing. Darcy confirmed she woke up and told him she'd been pushed but it was after having a nightmare. I'm still waiting for Forensics' report on the car but *if* she was pushed then that was the first attempt on her life. She's in hospital as a result of the second. Will they try again at the hospital? If so, why? What does she know that is bothering her attacker? Was it him ringing to find out where he stands?'

Pel removed his glasses and stared at Pujol, who was already preparing to bolt for his life.

'You've either got an over-active imagination,' he said, reaching for the packet of Gauloises, 'or you've got a brain lurking somewhere. Get over to the hospital immediately and don't leave Kate's bedside until someone relieves you.'

19

By six thirty Darcy had the house organised; he had Annie in the kitchen stirring strange-smelling things in saucepans and the boys nailed to the floor in front of a video he'd had the wits to hire. He was steaming behind a small glass of whisky at the table.

'What the hell are you cooking?' he growled, banging down his glass.

'Food,' Annie replied without looking round.

'It smells disgusting.'

'Look, mate, I didn't have to come and keep house for you, I did it because I like Kate and the boys – and you,' she added, brandishing a large wooden spoon, 'just a little bit. So, you'd better be nice to me, or I'll leave.'

'Sorry.'

'What's eating you,' she asked, slopping a tot of whisky into the bottom of a tumbler and sitting down opposite him, 'apart from the fact that Kate's in hospital miles away and you're stuck here with me and the boys?'

'It's not that.'

'Well, it should be!'

'Yes, it is, but it's something else as well.'

'Tell Auntie Annie, she's a good listener.'

Darcy took a gulp at his glass. It was none of her business but he told her anyway. 'Kate won't marry me and Cheriff was chatting her up.'

Annie hooted with laughter. 'Poor jealous man,' she said. 'Who cares if Kate won't marry you, you live with her, don't you? Everyone calls her Madame Darcy, what more do you want?'

'A ring on her finger and for Cheriff to leave her alone.'

'What difference would a ring make? Mark her as your possession, Monsieur Male Chauvinist Pig?'

'I'd wear one too.'

'So you could be her possession. Darcy,' Annie said softly, 'perhaps loving and being loved is enough. I know it is for me.'

'What do you know about it?'

'I'm loved by someone who will never marry me.'

'You've got a man in your life?' Darcy said, surprised. He'd only ever seen Annie Saxe, the Lion of Belfort, as one of the chaps. He'd never thought of her as a woman before.

'I'm not that repugnant.'

'No, of course you're not, that's not what I meant.' He looked at her as she rose from the table to stir her cauldron. He had to admit she was well made, long legs, neat little waist and everything else, it was all in the right place and well in proportion. He looked away. He didn't really like redheads but on her it seemed to work, and her flashing green eyes watching him now ... yes, she was a very attractive woman. He was startled.

'Yes, I'm sorry,' he said, 'you're actually very, well, you're very ...'

'Forget it, I'm not interested in compliments from you, it's my man that counts, as it does for Kate. Don't worry about Cheriff, he's already got his hands full.'

'I do worry about him. He offered to come back here again, it's as if he wants to encrust himself on Kate's life, and the boys adore him.'

'Kids like anyone who's nice to them, and he wants to be here because I'm here.'

'I beg your pardon?' Darcy took a good gulp at his glass.

'Don't you breathe a word, or I'll bash your brains in with my wooden spoon. We've kept it a secret for six months so far.'

'Why?'

'Because we work in the same team, Pel wouldn't appreciate it, and because he's Muslim, I'm Catholic. In his family the two don't mix.'

'Ring him.'

'What?'

'Ring him and tell him to come over.'

'No.'

'I want to go to the hospital and see Kate, I was rather short with her earlier. Tell him to come over, I don't want to leave you alone with the boys.'

'Why? Are you frightened I might break them too?' Annie grinned. 'The Lion of Belfort is being tamed, you know.'

When Darcy arrived in Kate's room he was very surprised to find Pujol the Puppy playing Scrabble with her.

'What are you doing here?' It seemed everyone had access to his lady.

'Pel's orders,' Pujol replied, leaping to attention. 'Received a phone call and decided it was better that someone stay here all the time.'

'What the hell are you blathering on about?'

'May I speak to you alone?'

'If you've got something to say, say it, here and now.'

'Yes, sir.'

'And don't call me sir.'

'No, sir – Darcy.'

'God, that's even worse,' he said, sighing. 'Never mind, what's all this about someone surveilling my wife, I mean Kate.'

Pujol explained. Kate went very pale.

'They killed my car, they may have killed my dog and they're still after me. Why don't they just go away? They must be mad,' she whispered, shivering. 'That's frightening, Darcy, they might manage it next time.'

'That's why we decided to protect you,' Pujol pointed out.

Kate was frowning and agitated, Scrabble letters were tumbling on to the floor like confetti. 'The van,' she said. 'The evening you were called to the rubbish dump to look for a chopped-up woman – remember? It was a hoax – do you think it was them who rang to keep you in town? I should have been driving Marie to Paris, but instead she took the train. We were both supposed to be away from the house so they could pass unseen, but I was there and I saw the driver of the van in the lane, the night Marie's house was cleared out. I only saw him in profile but I'm sure it was the same man before he shaved his beard off, the bearded man who raped Anita.' She stared at the two men in horror. 'That van was the van that pushed me off the road. Darcy!'

Misset was hiding in the sergeants' room the following morning when Nini came in through the main entrance to ask for him. The desk sergeant buzzed him but Misset said he wasn't in. Nosjean was coming in through the door from the hospital; he looked young and unhappy and he was wearing a pale pink shirt. Nini pounced. As Nosjean guided her up the stairs to Pel's office he was thinking of his wife – would it be today?

Pel was in no mood to receive ladies, but there was one standing in his office asking him to listen to stories about pink socks. Nosjean was going to pay for this later. He lit a cigarette and inhaled deeply. It didn't help, she was still there, telling him about the industrial estate now. He glanced up at her. She was holding a newspaper in her hand and pointing at the picture they'd released to the press, the one Kate and Debray had put together.

'The funny thing is, I haven't seen them for days.'

Pel's specs snapped back into place. 'When did you last see them?'

'Not long ago. They were loading furniture into their van. Same van as usual but they'd changed the sign on the side. I always thought that was odd, sometimes it was a removals firm, Démon Déménagement, other days it was Beau Brocante – you know, antiques that aren't quite old enough to be real antiques.'

'You got that, Nosjean? What's the address of this depot place, madame?'

'Do you know, I honestly couldn't say, but you can see it from my front door, perhaps you could pop over for a cup of tea and I could point it out for you?'

'Are you sure this is one of the men?' Pel asked.

'Pretty sure, although he had a beard, that's why I didn't recognise him at first.'

'What colour?'

'Sort of red, his hair was blondish though, quite dashing he was but better without it. I always find beards tickle, don't you?'

'Yes, quite. I don't suppose you know his name, do you?'

'Jean-Christophe, but everyone calls him JC.'

'That's it?'

'Well, yes, I called him JC, he called me Nini. We didn't bother with Monsieur and Madame, went straight into Christian names.'

Nini the Pink left, happy with her morning's work; she was looking forward to making tea for half a dozen policemen.

Pel looked at Nosjean after she'd gone. 'Misset was sitting in her house for well over a week. Get him in here. Get the papers drawn up with the Juge d'Instruction to go into that depot. Get four more men and two unmarked cars. Nosjean, you're coming with me. And,' he added, 'I think we'd better have guns.'

'Patron, could you find someone else to – '

'Nosjean,' Pel snapped, 'you're a policeman first and foremost, we'll find someone else after we've cleared this little affair up.'

Misset admitted having possibly seen the man in question, he also admitted that he'd seen the van, but he hadn't noticed they'd changed the signs or what they'd loaded or unloaded.

'Open your eyes,' Pel bellowed, 'plug your brain in. Holy Mother of God! I think your piles operation did for you!'

'Ingrowing toenails, sir.'

'Sod your toenails and your piles, sod the whole bloody lot of you, you idiot. What were you doing in that woman's house?'

'Drinking tea.'

'That's all.'

'Sir, she's completely potty, you do realise, don't you?'

'But she's not blind. Misset,' Pel sighed, trying to keep his temper, 'you'll be coming in one of the cars with us to go into that depot. You'll be carrying a gun, and you'll do exactly as you're told. Do you understand?'

As Misset closed the door behind him Pel was muttering, 'Perhaps he'll shoot himself, or get run down by a bus. Perhaps I should just strangle him with my bare hands.'

They were ready. Misset had gone in through the front door of Nini's house as usual. Pel, Nosjean, Cheriff, Bardolle and Pujol climbed inelegantly over the garden hedge, skirted round the strange pink swimming pool and were let in through the back door. The main road buzzed with traffic but at the front of the house all was quiet. The *zone industrielle* was full of parked cars but only the occasional lorry came and went. They stood behind the net curtains and watched. There was no sign of life in the depot. In the kitchen behind them Nini was brewing enough tea for a regiment.

The morning passed slowly. Everyone was sick of tea by the time midday chimed. Office workers began coming out to their cars and moving off for lunch. Soon the parking spaces were empty.

'We'll wait ten minutes,' Pel said, 'then if there's still no sign of life you move into position.'

At half-past twelve Nini was alone drinking tea; the six policemen had left via the garden and were now posted round the depot.

Nosjean banged at the metal door. There was no reply. Pel nodded; Bardolle braced himself against Cheriff's back and lifted his foot ready to kick the door in.

As it collapsed three of them ran in, guns drawn, and waited. Nothing moved. Pel went in looking puzzled. 'Search the place,' he said. After another half-hour they knew the hangar was not housing their two criminals. In fact it wasn't housing anything, no van, no furniture, just a bit of rubbish flapping about on the floor.

20

So that was it. They'd missed them, if they'd ever been there. Perhaps Nini the Pink was potty after all. Pel ordered his men back to the office and wandered across to see her with Pujol in tow; he didn't want to let the new boy out of sight.

She was sitting happily at her window sipping tea when they arrived. As they were served with fresh cups and saucers Pel asked her again about the two men she'd seen. She repeated what she'd told them, adding nothing and leaving nothing out. Either she'd rehearsed it well or it was the truth.

'Why did you take so much interest in them?' he asked at last.

'Because they were quite handsome, especially the taller one, but it didn't matter which – I'm looking for a husband, you see.'

Pel raised his eyebrows. 'It's difficult bringing up two girls on my own,' she explained. 'I get fed up with going to bed at eight o'clock and having no one to talk to. I can't go out because I've nobody to look after my girls, I'm not leaving them with strangers.'

'But you told me you invited one of these men into the house,' Pel pointed out.

'That's different.'

'Madame, it's time I informed you that these two men may be dangerous.'

'They didn't look it, JC was perfectly charming.'

Pel sighed, drained his cup and rose to go. 'If they come back please contact me,' he said, dropping a card on the table, 'day or night. And', he added, 'I would advise you not to invite either of them into the house again.'

When Pel arrived back at the Hôtel de Police he found Dr Cham waiting for him.

'Good news or bad news?' he asked.

'Neither, a puzzle.'

'I've got enough of those, thank you, but I expect one more won't make much difference. Pull up a chair and let me have it.' He liked Cham, he was worth listening to.

'It's only an idea,' the doctor explained, folding his two metres into sitting position. 'Boudet dropped in on me late last night. He'd been thinking about the Claudine Bonnet murder. He cited the case of an Englishwoman, in Yorkshire to be precise, who died having fallen on to a pair of trimming scissors while decorating the staircase.'

'Claudine Bonnet was not decorating the staircase.'

'No, but the footprint on the table was hers.'

'Get on with it, what have you and Boudet cooked up?'

'Well, he went to the scene of the crime the night Claudine Bonnet's body was found and after that he was stuck in the lab with me because of the snow. It was a hilarious twelve hours.'

'So you said.'

'Yes, but before the hilarity started he assisted me with the autopsy – we had nothing else to do stuck there so we got on with it. He remarked then that although she had many deep cuts from the bottle she'd fallen on, she only had one knife wound. It's not unknown but it's unusual – one expects in the case of a death by stabbing at least two penetrations, to be sure so to speak. One penetration indicates a stabbing in anger but not premeditated murder.'

'Or the murderer was an amateur without your experience and believed one good hole would be enough.'

'Well, yes, I suppose so, but as a scientist I work from statistics and known facts. However, I must confess we have been guessing. Boudet put forward a hypothesis that was very interesting.'

'The suspense is killing me.' Pel sighed and reached for his cigarettes. Cham was getting as bad as Leguyader, with the help of Boudet he could become worse.

'Let's go back to the beginning, forget a second party and let's say she was alone and drinking. She picked at the food she'd prepared – that we know from the stomach contents. From the blood test we know she was drunk. Alcohol accentuates one's mood, if you're feeling jolly, it makes you more jolly, if you're feeling miserable, *idem*, it makes you more miserable. Alone for a week since her husband disappeared, she was probably feeling very miserable, particularly as it was Christmas. For some reason she climbs on to the table and picks up a knife.'

'What the hell for?'

'I have no idea.'

'So your theory ends there,' Pel said hopefully.

'I'm afraid it's only just started. So she's on the table with a knife in her hand,' Cham went on hurriedly, 'scattering food, glasses and the wine bottle and,' he said, 'this is important, the vinaigrette.'

'But what was she doing on the table, apart from perhaps dancing for her male friend, i.e. her murderer.'

'But if there was no one else, she was up there for another reason, I can't tell you why. Anyway, she slips in the oily vinaigrette and falls off the table, bangs her head on a log and impales herself on the knife, while a bottle of *vin cuit* smashes underneath her. She's dazed and drunk, she realises she's bleeding and discovers the knife implanted in the upper part of her right breast piercing the innominate artery. Unfortunately, the reaction of most people when they find themselves in this situation is to pluck out the offending object, and it's the worst possible reaction. The hole is no longer bunged and profuse bleeding commences. Try it with a plastic bottle filled with water and a skewer. While the skewer remains piercing the plastic only a little water seeps out but the moment you

remove the skewer you have a small but veritable waterfall.'
Cham looked up at Pel, who was fiddling with his files. 'It's
only an idea . . .'

'So you keep saying.' Pel reached for another cigarette.

'If she removed the knife she effectively killed herself. Her
blood would have been pumped by her continually beating
heart on to the floor in quantity, although of course it became
weaker as time passed. Shock plus her advanced state of
inebriation would have prevented her from calling for help
but in any case she would have lost consciousness pretty
rapidly.'

Pel was feeling queasy. He got up and paced round the
room.

'But this is all a hypothesis?' he said.

'Only that. We can't prove it – Boudet was hoping you
might be able to.'

'You're as potty as the Pink,' Pel replied. 'Tell Boudet I
forbid him to spend the night locked in the lab with you ever
again. He deals too much in blood and guts, I get the feeling
he enjoys it sometimes. He's as obsessed as you are. Now get
out, Cham, and let me get on with something serious.'

'One last thing. Boudet thinks your rapist is a madman,
capable of anything, not an ordinary criminal – someone
unpredictable, highly dangerous. Seeing his patient beaten up
like that quite obviously upset him.'

Pel returned to his files on Brigitte Breille and Anita
Tabeyse, the two rape victims, and the JC connection, the
handsome removal man on the industrial estate. A smiling
nutter intent on revenge? He passed a hand through his
thinning hair; it was all getting very complicated. Pel breathed
Gauloise and considered the possibilities. He was going to
swallow his pride and suffer some expert advice before he
worked out their next move.

Darcy was working things out too. He was sitting staring at
the files concerning the robberies and the van Kate had seen

in the lane. He wanted to find the driver, and fast, before Kate's life was put in danger again. The robberies – the Breille house where Brigitte had been raped, Marie's house just down the lane from where he lived, plus the half-dozen others that had occurred since the beginning of September – had been investigated so far perfectly efficiently by Bardolle and Brochard. He left his office to hunt one of them down. Brochard was nowhere to be seen but he found Bardolle in the sergeants' room typing with two fingers and his tongue between his teeth. He was a massive man, their very own Hulk, who managed with difficulty to operate a typewriter with hands like shovels.

'Looks like hard work,' he said.

Bardolle was relieved to be interrupted. 'Every time I bash one key three or four hammers get locked together,' he replied, mopping his brow.

'Try the electric one.'

Bardolle laughed. 'That's even worse. I get a string of letters appearing on the page – it looks like Chinese. I spend more time rubbing out than typing and when I've finished the Patron complains about all the holes in my report.'

'Get Pujol or Rigal to do it,' Darcy suggested.

'They've already got enough to type for the rest of the year.'

'You still on the robberies?'

'That's what I'm doing at the moment.'

'What have you come up with?'

'Not a lot. We've got some fingerprints but none with criminal records, they're all family and friends. Forensics even managed to piece together a broken ornament to get one fingerprint, but it was of no help.'

Darcy left Bardolle to his heavy-handed typing and went down to see Debray playing on his computer. He stood for a while watching him manipulate the magic machine to produce photographs, fingerprints and information. As he paused to paw over the paperwork beside him, Darcy asked him about the information he had on the robberies.

'Just collating it,' Debray said, pressing a couple of buttons. 'Want to see it?'

He took Darcy through a number of menus until he found what he was looking for. 'This is the abridged version,' he said, 'the titles under which the rest of the stuff is kept.'

They looked through it together, watching the screen change under Debray's command until it finally went blank.

'That's it,' he said. 'Nothing very helpful, I'm afraid. I've got one more little game to play if you'd like to stay and watch.'

A fingerprint appeared on one half of the screen and after a couple of seconds another one appeared next to it: they were the same.

'The one on the left was taken from the broken ornament,' Debray explained, 'the one on the right is a house owner. I made a search to see if I could find the same fingerprint anywhere in the robbery document. It's not a known criminal, you see.'

Darcy was losing interest. 'So it was the owner of the ornament who dropped it – it happens.'

Debray was frantically pressing buttons again as Darcy turned to leave.

'Wait!'

'Oh, come on, Debray, I haven't got time to watch your pretty pictures all day.'

'But the fingerprint on the ornament matches Christian Dolle, your ex-next-door neighbour.'

'So he was careless.'

'The ornament was in the Breille house.'

Leguyader was surprised to find Pel in his forensic laboratory. 'What can I solve for you this time?' he asked smugly. Pel immediately regretted being there: the scientist's attitude was enough to drive him to drink, and knowing smoking was absolutely forbidden in the lab, he had an urgent need to drag on a Gauloise.

'Can you give me an opinion,' he asked carefully, 'instead of a quotation or a list of statistics?'

'I doubt it.'

Pel sighed, fingered the inviting blue packet in his pocket and pressed on. 'It has been suggested', he said, 'that the rapist on our patch is deranged. What do you think?'

Leguyader put his hands together and leant his elbows on his desk. It was just was Pel was dreading. It was going to be a long answer.

'All rapists are deranged, more or less,' the scientist explained. 'They have either social, mental or sexual problems, sometimes all three. They are unstable pathetic members of our society from whom the public should be protected. The only way of doing that is to put them where there is no public, that is, behind locked doors, then throw away the key.'

'Is that a quotation?'

'No, that's what you asked for, my opinion.'

Pel finally lit a cigarette while thinking about what he'd heard. Leguyader started flapping his arms, which made him look as if he was trying to fly out of his chair. Pel puffed soothingly, unaware of the panic he was causing.

'For crying out loud, man, you can't smoke in here! Come into the corridor with your suicide stick.'

Pel followed him out. 'Is our man capable of murder?'

'Very likely. Most of them end up killing, it's almost inevitable even if it's not deliberate. They get carried away, or a woman defends herself too well and they retaliate.

'In 1959 a rapist called Pommerencke pushed a struggling girl out of a train, pulled the communication cord, then leapt out to rape her and finally stab her to death. He started by molesting, went on to rape and ended up a murderer. When he was arrested in 1960 he was charged with ten murders with rape, twenty simple rapes plus thirty-five assaults and burglaries. He was sentenced to one hundred and forty years in prison.'

Pel was digesting this information while lighting another cigarette.

'Shall I go on?'

Pel nodded from behind a cloud of smoke.

'Kurten, another German, was a great admirer of Jack the Ripper. He was stimulated by the sight of blood and the humiliation of his victims. He was a sexual sadist who, his wife claimed, was a good religious man and loved his children. He was guillotined.'

'But that was in Germany,' Pel pointed out.

'What difference does it make? Jack the Ripper wasn't and the murders at 10 Rillington Place were in England. A Special Constable in the War Reserve Police raped and killed six women – he was hanged in 1953. During his teens he'd been nicknamed Reggie-no-dick.'

'English.'

Leguyader sighed. 'Vacher was French. He was committed to an asylum as mentally unstable but was released after a year apparently cured. In three and a half years he then murdered seven women and four youths. Cutting and raping were his specialities. He claimed he was insane but after many months the experts declared him to be sane. He was tried and guillotined.'

'A long time ago, then.'

'At the turn of the century.'

'Holy Mother of God!' Pel exclaimed, throwing down his cigarette and grinding it into the floor. 'The human being hasn't made much progress, has it?'

Leguyader was watching the spreading blackened tobacco on the shining white-tiled floor. 'No,' he agreed sadly, 'man doesn't change much as time passes, he just gets more so.'

Pel frowned. 'What do you mean, more so?'

'Faster, greedier, more stupid, more violent. Like your rapist – he'll go on trying to fulfil his appetite for whatever it is he feeds on, and eventually he'll succeed in killing someone. He's considered it already, *n'est-ce pas*? From the state of the house when the forensic team arrived, I'd say Madame Darcy narrowly escaped being murder victim number one.'

Pel was turning slowly to wander off down the corridor. He was lighting another cigarette.

'It was a pleasure,' Leguyader shouted after him. 'Don't bother to thank me for my time, precious though it is. Next time you want an opinion I'll hand you the books and you can look it up yourself.' But Pel was gone.

'Ungrateful little bugger,' he muttered and slammed the lab door behind him.

21

Pel frowned all the way back to his office. He was still frowning when Darcy told him about the fingerprint match they'd been able to make from the ornament in the Breille house. He wasn't impressed. 'We've got a face with no record and a fingerprint with a name, but the face and the fingerprint don't go together. Both the face and the owner of the finger-print have disappeared – I need more, Darcy, much more. Don't come back until you have it.'

Darcy had an idea where more might be available: Marie. After all, it was her husband's fingerprint they'd found. Unfortunately, they had no address for her since she'd gone to Paris with Pierrot. He didn't know her maiden name so he couldn't even find her mother in the Minitel listings. He'd never been told Pierrot's surname, but he remembered thinking his face was familiar. Now would be a good time to check.

He waded his way through the mug shots, full face and profile with their prison number underneath. He could easily be wasting his time, a whole afternoon was a lot in a policeman's life, but it was worth a try. He was getting bored by six o'clock, but at six thirty he said, 'Eureka' and looked through Pierrot's dossier.

'Pierrot Penne, born 11.2.50, Lyons, carpenter, married twice, divorced twice, four children. Granted custody of two youngest. Convicted of robbery, 10.10.84, condemned to five years' imprisonment, served three. Released 20.11.87. Present address 3 rue de la Violette, Paris. No further recommendations.' That meant he was neither convicted nor suspected of anything since. He was clean; in eighteen months' time he'd be able to vote again and leave the country if he wished, a normal citizen, except for the Social Security number he'd carry all his life. In the old days they branded criminals with hot irons or cut off an ear; today with civilisation they simply prefixed your Social Security number with 29. The result was the same, anyone in authority would know he'd served a prison sentence. But who cared? Darcy had found him, in theory.

It was too late to phone that evening, but the following morning he got through to the Paris Police Judiciaire, waiting while he was passed from one department to another. He finally spoke to a hard-working imbecile like himself who was prepared to help. At long last it was confirmed that Pierrot Penne was still at 3 rue de la Violette, and he had a telephone number.

'Do you want us to pick him up?' the Paris detective asked.

'No, I only want to talk to him.'

'What's he done? Let me in on it.'

'As far as I know he's done nothing since his release in 1987, I just want to talk to him in connection with some of his friends. Don't hassle him, he doesn't deserve it, yet.'

'Let me know if you need help.'

'*Entendu.*'

Darcy dialled the number he'd been given, hoping it would be Marie who answered. It wasn't.

'*Oui*, this is Pierrot, who's calling?'

'Daniel Darcy. We met when Marie discovered her house had been cleaned out.'

'Ah, *le flic.*'

Darcy reluctantly agreed he was.

'Marie says you're okay, any friend of hers is a friend of mine, as long as you're not after me.'

'*Non*, Pierrot, it's not you I want. I'll admit I went through records to find you but only so I could speak to Marie – it could be important.'

'She's not in, but I'll get her to ring you as soon as she gets back. Shouldn't be long. What's your number, mate?'

Darcy expected to have to wait all day, if not all week, and was happily surprised when half an hour later Marie was on the line asking to speak to him. Her first question was to ask if Kate and the boys were well. Darcy explained rapidly what had happened, slightly taken aback that she didn't already know.

'I don't read the newspapers,' she explained. 'I don't even watch the telly much, except *Les Feux de l'Amour* after lunch. It helps put me and the kids to sleep for a *sieste*.'

'So you haven't seen the description of the man we're looking for? I'll read it to you, tell me if you recognise him.'

He hadn't really expected to hit the jackpot, but it had been worth trying.

'No, it doesn't mean a thing, Daniel. What's it all about?'

'He's our prime suspect for a number of crimes. He may be working with your ex-husband.'

'Christian? The creep, it doesn't surprise me he's turned into a common thief. Look, I'm ever so sorry about Kate, I'll do anything I can to help. We were thinking of coming back to the country. Paris is driving us mad, and Pierrot would like his kids to have a garden to play in. Perhaps this is the moment. When Kate comes out of hospital I can lend a hand. She was lovely to me, I owe her.'

'If you happen to be there I'm sure she'll be grateful,' Darcy said, 'but more importantly, has Christian been in contact?'

'He rang my mother, and she told him to get lost. She tells him that every time.'

'So he'll ring again.'

'It's likely, he's grovelling and apologising, wanting to come back. Sod him – I don't need to have my face mashed every other day.'

'Marie, the next time he rings get a phone number, tell him you're finally reconsidering, tell him anything, but find out where he is.'

'I'll try.'

'It's important, Marie, and urgent.'

'Has he got something to do with what happened to Kate?'

'That's what I'd like to find out.'

'What do I do when I've got the phone number?'

'Ring me immediately.'

'*D'accord*. When's Kate coming out of hospital?'

'Any day now, I hope.'

'Don't be surprised if you find a light on in my house then. I think that's the deciding factor, we're coming home. We've hardly got any furniture, but who needs it when we've got friends.' The line went dead, leaving Darcy staring at the phone and smiling.

The following morning the newspapers published an account of the burglaries, the rapes and the attempt on Kate's life together with the names of Christian Dolle and JC who were believed to have rented a depot on the *zone industrielle*. Journalists were showing renewed interest as a result of the computer portrait they'd been given. The police had released it in the hope of someone recognising the man even though they knew only too well that it would also attract all sorts of time-wasters into the Hôtel de Police and that millions more would phone, all claiming to have seen JC, and each one would have to be followed up just in case it was genuine. Extra phones were installed while sleeves were rolled up in preparation for the onslaught.

'Jesus, they've got two names and a photo of you, how did they do that?'

JC, who was still lying on his stomach, snatched the newspaper. 'It's not a very good likeness now I've got a bit of stubble on my chin. You'll have to get me some black hair dye, then it'll be useless. I wonder who gave them all this stuff. It couldn't be the *flic*'s wife, she already coughed up all she knew a couple of days ago.'

'Then who?'

JC was thinking hard. 'Hang on a minute,' he said. 'The bit of pink fluff on the industrial estate, you reckon it's her?'

'You went into her house, not me. Surely you didn't bloody tell her our names, did you?'

But JC denied it. 'No, of course not, it must have been when she came over to ask us in for a cup of tea that evening. She could have been listening at the door while we were unloading, she must've heard our names then. I bet that bloke with the dark glasses was a copper, and I was dumb enough to think it was her boyfriend. Now I think about it, he came in the morning and left in the evening, if you're bonking someone it's usually the other way round. He looked stupid enough to be a copper. We're going to have to shut her up before she remembers anything else. But we're going to have to be careful.'

'Maybe we should pack it in and disappear before we're in too deep.'

'You're joking, we've only just started, the money's on its way. This is the third time I've worked the triangle, it never fails, the stuff's impossible to trace. The antiques are in Marseille, the silver's over the border in Switzerland and the rest, well, if we can't get rid of it here we'll take it into Italy, they'll buy anything. No, we've got a few more deals to do before we pack it in, and then only temporarily. This beats working for a living any day. Soon we'll be off on our hols, then we'll work a different area for a couple of months and off for the summer. They'll never catch us, we're all over the place and nowhere.'

'But they've got our names.'

'They've got yours,' JC pointed out. 'Just call yourself something else.' He thought for a moment. 'How about Luc, yeah, Luc Buc, short and simple,' he suggested, laughing, 'like you.'

22

The snow had gone but the wind was still bitterly cold. The police arrived for the day well wrapped and rubbing their hands together; however, the heating was back to normal and they could now work without overcoats and plumbers to obstruct them. All they had to worry about was their Patron, the inscrutable Monsieur Pel: he was worse than the weather, his stare was colder than the snow, his bite was worse than the wind and his moods were worse than the black clouds that insisted on hovering overhead. Until they had at least the rape cases sorted out it wasn't going to change. Public opinion in the city had the police force by the short and curlies; they wanted results, they wanted the man behind bars, they didn't feel safe, they wanted action. The police were prepared to give them all the action they wanted – trouble was, it wasn't producing the results. They could wear their legs down to stumps but nothing changed.

Pel looked like a thunderstorm with lightning on its way as they filed into the morning meeting. When they came out forty minutes later they felt windswept and battered; lightning had struck. Misset in particular had been feeling the heat. Pel had ordered him back to Nini the Pink's house permanently in case Christian and/or JC turned up. He'd also ordered him to remove his stupid sun-glasses and plug his brain in. The rest of the team hadn't laughed in front of Pel but they were laughing now.

Misset bypassed the sergeants' room where the phones were ringing non-stop and went straight out into the street.

Pujol and Rigal were still fielding the million sightings of their two wanted men: they'd been seen in the supermarket at Talant and drinking coffee on their way to Paris, and a poor old dear who was obviously completely batty was sure they'd been stealing plants from her garden. Each call was followed up and a number of arrests were made, but Christian and JC were still at large.

But Pel had something else on his mind. He told Darcy to tell Angelface Aimedieu to bring round the car and to meet him outside. The moment he was installed beside Angelface he regretted it. His choir-boy face hid a devilish driver; Pel was petrified as he weaved in and out of the city traffic, screeching to a halt at the traffic lights, winking at any pretty girl that passed and whizzing off at top speed to impress them. By the time they arrived outside the Bonnet house Pel was a nervous wreck. He staggered from the car mopping his brow and lighting a much-needed cigarette with shaking fingers. Darcy was grinning; Angelface adjusted his tie, smoothed his hair and dropped the car keys neatly in his jacket pocket.

'I'll drive on the way back,' Pel growled.

'We'll take the bus then, Patron,' Angelface said sweetly. He opened the garden gate and bowed as Pel passed through it.

'Cheeky child,' Pel muttered. 'Why the hell you're a police-man beats me.'

'The moment I'm discovered I'll be off.'

Pel scowled, the man was talking gibberish.

'He still wants to be an actor, Patron,' Darcy explained, opening the door to the house. 'What is it we're looking for?'

'A reason for being on the table.'

Darcy and Angelface glanced at each other and followed their boss into the main room. Nothing much had changed. No one had been in to clear up, it still looked as if someone had held a ten-round boxing match in there. The only things that were missing were Claudine's body and the smell, which was at least a slight improvement. They stood staring at the

158

debris, the cold fireplace, the empty bottles, the wreck that had once been a home.

'Boudet and Cham came up with the idea and I'm checking it out. I think they are both as mad as hatters, but as professionals we must cover all possibilities,' Pel explained. 'They suggested that she fell from the table on to a knife. What we've got to do is find out why she was up there, if she was up there for any other purpose than dancing a jig for her murderer. Personally, I think it's a crazy idea but we're obliged to follow it up.'

They wandered round the room looking for inspiration rather than for evidence. It was a sad room: the feeling of death still lingered, the small Christmas tree on the sideboard had shed its needles, the baubles and tinsel hung limply waiting to be discarded. Aimedieu stepped on a festive card lying on the floor by the table and, picking it up, read the inscription: 'Joyeux Noël et Bonne Année, Jacques et Lillianne.'

'The other half of Leisure Pleasure,' Darcy said, picking up another; looking up, he saw a string of them attached to the beam. He counted them: there were seven more. 'They didn't have many friends and relations,' he commented. 'I wonder who'll inherit the house?'

He was still staring at the cards as Pel flicked his dying cigarette into the fireplace. 'Darcy, Christmas is over. I don't care about the friends and relations unless they murdered her. Now get on with the job.'

'How tall was Claudine Bonnet?'

'I can't remember, what difference does it make?'

'I'm not sure,' Darcy replied, slowly wandering round the room, 'but you know, if I was all alone for Christmas I wouldn't bother to decorate the house.'

'Maybe she was expecting her husband back at any minute,' Aimedieu suggested. 'That's why she made the effort.'

'He didn't come back, he was outside all the time frozen under a pile of logs, poor bugger, not that she knew it.'

'For the moment we'll concentrate on Claudine, not her husband,' Pel interrupted impatiently.

'I know,' Darcy replied, fingering the dead Christmas tree, 'but I was just thinking, if everyone else was busy celebrating and looking forward to the New Year and I was still on my own, I'd burn the bloody tree and rip down the rest, cards and all.' He went back to the lonely little string of cards then, climbing on to the table, he reached up to pluck a couple off. He could just reach the beam.

'Darcy what the – '

'Patron, if Claudine was shorter than me then I think I've found your answer.'

Misset was sulking. He'd sulked all morning as he wandered round the city looking for an excuse not to go back to Nini the Pink. He'd stopped for lunch and dallied a long time before finally setting off in the direction of the industrial estate. He was going to go back into the depot and find something, something important, he told himself – that would show Pel, that would shut him up, he'd have to give him his dark glasses back then.

As Misset poked about in the corners of the empty depot, Pel, Aimedieu and Darcy were comparing notes.

'So that's it. Madame was not murdered,' Aimedieu announced gaily, 'she killed herself by accident.'

'So it seems,' Pel replied, studying the file in front of him. 'I was convinced Cham and Boudet cooked this thing up as a joke. But it fits – as Darcy suggests, she may have climbed up to untie the cards and not been able to, being shorter than him – which is not surprising, most people are shorter than him.'

'Our stately Arab, Cheriff Kader Camel, is taller,' Aimedieu pointed out.

'He's the exception to everything.' Pel scowled. Being reminded of everyone's height was not a conversation he wanted to indulge in; he was shorter than the whole team, and balder. 'As I was saying, she couldn't untie the string so she picked up a knife off the table and started slashing at it.

The marks on the beam indicate that; it only remains for Forensics to prove it. Sloshed and slashing she slips in the spilt vinaigrette and falls on the knife she's holding, bashing her head on the way down. She plucks out the offending knife, throws it away, it falls in the fire, end of story.' Pel sighed. He hoped like hell Forensics would prove it, it would be one less murder. There was always her husband, frozen under the log pile.

Finally Pel closed the file. Forensics had confirmed it. Leguyader had been, seen and proved it. He was delighted to be the shining light in Pel's life and to show him that, without his department, Pel's department would be permanently fumbling about in the wrong direction. He'd taken the afternoon to collect the proof and analyse it and until seven twenty-five to explain it. He was ecstatic. Pel hated him. He was going home.

Misset had long finished poking about at the depot. He'd found nothing and had taken his disappointment to be consoled in a bar where he dismally watched children come home from school and eventually the stream of cars as the office workers did the same. He hung about a bit more – if he went home he would find his wife, overweight and angry, his numerous adolescent offspring and his mother-in-law who resembled an all-in wrestler and didn't look as if she was ever going back to her own home.

As he ordered a whisky – what the hell, he wasn't driving, just a short walk to marital bliss – the door bell was ringing at Nini the Pink's. Her daughters were in their bedroom doing their homework. She also thought, what the hell, and opened the door.

Half an hour later the two little girls were huddled in their cupboard sobbing silently; through the thin walls of the house they could hear someone trying to murder their mother.

23

As usual Pujol had been quietly sitting in Kate's room until a young uniformed policeman arrived to relieve him for the night duty; he had his instructions and Pujol left the hospital. After a couple of hours the young policeman asked Kate if he could go and get a cup of coffee to help keep him awake, he'd only be away a minute or two.

Kate was feeling happy, she'd been given the all-clear, tomorrow she'd be going home, so she told him to take half an hour if necessary, she'd be fine.

Coming into the hospital was a man who, with a certain amount of encouragement, had learned to blame her for his loneliness. He wanted to see her, only briefly but it was important. As he took the lift up to her floor, a car drew up in a parking space outside. The occupants also asked at Acceuil for Kate's room number and they waited for the lift to come back down. When they finally arrived on the third floor they scoured the numerous signs to know in which direction they should go. At last outside Kate's door they stopped, grinned and went in.

'Surprise!'

Kate was on the floor fighting; a hand clasping a piece of cloth smothered her mouth to stop her screaming. The light reflected suddenly off the edge of the knife coming down towards her.

Pel and Darcy got the call almost simultaneously, Pel because he was in charge of things like murder and Darcy because he was Kate's husband, and Pel's right-hand man. Pel rose rapidly from his comfortable armchair, kissed his wife good-bye for the second time that day and went out into the bitter night. Darcy leapt from the table where he was sitting with Cheriff, Annie and the boys, dropped the phone, shouted at them to cope and fled for the car.

They arrived at the hospital entrance at the same time. Neither said a word as they ran for the lift. Inside, they finally drew breath.

'Who's dead?' Darcy panted.

'Someone having a go at Kate.'

The lift stopped and they hurried down the corridor to her room. There were already two uniformed policemen standing outside; one was looking sheepish and said nothing, the other one asked them for identification. They flashed their badges and went in. Kate was sitting on the bed beside Marie, who was staring at her ex-husband, Christian Dolle, lying like a broken rag doll in the corner. Pierrot was sitting with his head in his hands.

'Kate!' Darcy sprang to her side, Marie went to Pierrot. Pel wondered where the hell he should start.

'He was trying to murder me,' Kate said at last. 'Pierrot stopped him.'

'I didn't mean to kill him.'

Pel called order to the proceeding. 'Kate, are you all right?'

'Just dazed,' she replied, hanging on to Darcy.

'You were the only one here all the time, so you'd better start.'

'He came in,' she said. 'I didn't shout because I knew him. He said he wanted news of Marie, wanted her to forgive him, that's the way the conversation started, so I told him to sit down. He came towards the bed. He had something in his hand – stupidly I thought he'd been crying and that it was a handkerchief, but it smelt strange. Then he started saying it was all my fault that Marie had left him and he lunged for the bed; next thing I knew we were both on the floor and I was fighting for my life again.'

'He had a knife in his other hand,' Marie continued. 'We came in without knocking to give Kate a surprise and found him holding her down. Pierrot didn't stop to think, he plucked him off and threw him across the room, and that was that.'

'I just wanted to get him off Kate,' Pierrot said, looking up, 'but he hardly weighed anything, he went flying.'

Christian Dolle was definitely dead; his neck had snapped as he hit the corner of the room. When the body had been removed and all the statements had been taken Darcy invited Pierrot and Marie back to Kate's house – it was the least he could do, he'd saved her life. Kate went home that night too. She felt safer away from the hospital with friends around her.

Pel went into the corridor to find out who was supposed to have been on guard. He was going to have their guts for garters.

Pujol, having been dismissed from his night duty at the hospital, had gone straight home to his bedsit, where he studied his notes on all the current cases blissfully unaware of the excitement at the hospital. He wasn't at all sure that he'd made the right decision joining the police force and wondered if being an insurance salesman would have been easier – less exciting, he thought, but more stable.

It was his habit to take the car and cruise round the city after dark, as he'd seen the American cops doing on the television, and it was while he was cruising that he passed the entrance to the *zone industrielle* and noticed a light still burning at Nini the Pink's house. She'd said she went to bed around eight; he looked at the car clock, ten minutes past ten. Odd, he thought.

When the door bell wasn't answered he cautiously glanced through the front window. Within seconds the call had gone through for an ambulance and the police but it was a good ten minutes later that he heard the faint sobbing coming from one of the bedrooms.

*

Nini the Pink had been knocked unconscious and left for dead, but she'd gone down fighting. She'd been stabbed a dozen times but astonishingly she was still alive. Her arms, breasts, thighs and stomach had holes in them, but nothing that couldn't be mended. The following morning she was sitting up in bed demanding a pot of tea. Pujol arrived with Pel to find her smiling.

'It's my chubbiness,' she explained to them, sipping delicately at her cup. 'You need a long knife to get through the six inches of flab to the vital organs. It's a shame he didn't get it right and remove ten kilos of ugly fat instead of just slicing the outer coating. Still, never mind,' she said cheerfully, 'now I'm here I can go on a diet. Where are the girls?'

Driving back through the city, Pujol didn't say a word. Out of the corner of his eye he could see his boss frowning heavily. Pel was deep in thought. Nini the Pink had been extraordinarily lucky, and she hadn't been raped; perhaps, as Leguyader had suggested, their lunatic had developed a taste for cutting instead of thrusting. He'd been right on one thing, it was getting worse. They had the necessary proof from the identification made by Kate, Anita Tabeyse and now Nini, together with the semen comparison from the two rape cases; the blood group was the same as that of the piece of flesh found in Rasputin's mouth. JC was responsible for all four attacks and the robbery at the Breille house. It was highly likely that with the help of Christian he was also responsible for the emptying of Marie's house and possibly the other robberies they had on file. It was a long list, and Pel didn't want it to get any longer. The next time he might succeed in killing someone – so far it was only his partner, Marie's ex-husband, who had gone to the morgue.

Pujol dropped his boss at the door of the Hôtel de Police, then went to the nearest florist's where he bought half a dozen pink roses.

Darcy arrived and made straight for Pel's office. It was

already nearly eleven o'clock and his absence had been noticed.

'Just because Kate's home you've got no excuse for being late,' Pel snapped, but he didn't look as cross as he sounded, although it was hard to tell, he hid it well behind his glasses and a curtain of smoke.

Darcy sat down in front of Pel's desk and helped himself from his packet of cigarettes.

'Not even if I know what Christian Dolle and JC were up to?' he asked.

Pel pushed his glasses up into his sparse hair, which looked like skid marks on a wet road. He turned his attention to Darcy and listened, forgetting to tick him off for pinching a precious Gauloise.

'Marie admitted she told her ex-husband that Kate was taking her to Paris to her mum's the night her cottage was cleaned out. He rang our house while Kate was up the lane with Rasputin. It was them that Kate saw that evening, which is why they've been trying to get rid of her ever since. They'd been working something JC called the triangle. They stole in one department and sold in three different places, often taking the small stuff over the borders into Belgium, Germany, Switzerland and Italy. At the end of August JC had told Christian he'd been working the triangle for over a year and the operation was getting too big for him alone, he needed a partner. Christian, being often out of work, readily joined him.'

'Was he in on the rapes?'

'No, but he was a weak man and easily influenced by bullies; apparently it was one of the main reasons he was always losing his job. As usual he latched on to someone he thought was powerful but this time it was a monster and he got trodden on.'

'Who told you about the triangle operation?' Pel asked.

'Christian rang Marie's mother yesterday afternoon. As instructed, she said Marie was unhappy without him and was ready to talk about trying again. She got a phone number off

166

him and Marie rang back. He told her everything, adding that soon it would be over, he just had one more thing to finish off. That one thing was Kate.'

'They were both here yesterday night,' Pel sighed, realising that Darcy's absence meant he didn't yet know of the attack made on Nini the Pink. 'While we were dealing with Kate, JC was dealing with the Pink.'

'Did he kill her?'

'No, she's very much alive and still drinking tea.'

'Patron, does Sarrazin have the story of her survival?'

'Not yet.'

'I think we should give it to him with everything else we know about the triangle operation, as JC calls it.'

'That would put her life in danger all over again.'

'Exactly.'

The Chief was against it. 'Imagine the public's opinion of the Police Judiciaire if it goes wrong. You're inviting the rapist back to have another go. No, it's too dangerous – and in a hospital too, you must be mad.'

Pel insisted. 'No, he's the madman, and getting more dangerous as the days slip by. There have been cases like him in the past and even knowing what they look like, their names and their family histories, sometimes it's taken years to trap them – and', he added ominously, 'they always leave a shocking trail of victims behind them. So far he hasn't succeeded in killing anyone, but the expert opinion is that it's inevitable, then we'll be picking up bodies all over France.'

The Chief wasn't convinced. 'If he had any sense he'd get out of the country while he's still got his freedom.'

'But he's not rational. He's deranged and if the idea of escape occurs to him we'll lose him until victims appear in Belgium, Germany, Switzerland or Italy. We can't be responsible for allowing him to continue.'

'How do you propose to protect the Pink?' the Chief finally

167

asked. Pel knew he was giving in, but he was the least of their troubles. After the Chief came the Procureur and the Juge d'Instruction, and of course they still had to have the Pink's co-operation.

At last the Chief asked to see the Procureur and the Juge d'Instruction. Pel went with him. Towards the end of the afternoon they left the Procureur's office with Madame Casteou, their favourite Juge d'Instruction.

'When's all this going to happen?' she asked as they walked down the corridor.

'As soon as possible. Twenty-four hours is our limit for getting the story into the papers, then all we can do is wait and hope.'

'Don't forget your bait must be moved to a small private clinic, the risk element must be reduced to negligible. Good luck.' She left them outside the building and headed for her car.

'That was surprisingly easy,' the Chief commented to Pel as they made their way back to the office.

'Three against one, the Procureur could hardly refuse,' Pel pointed out.

'It was a bit of luck having Casteou on our side. If it had been old Brisard we'd still be haggling.'

'Luck wasn't in it, Chief. I rang her and asked her to be present before Brisard got wind of what was going on.'

'You're a clever little bugger, aren't you?'

'I'm efficient,' Pel admitted. 'I just hope to God it works and we haven't lost him. My main worry is that he'll see the story but lie low long enough for us to call it off. Then he'll be back to see the Pink when we won't be watching – we can't protect her forever.'

'Perhaps it would be better not to publish what we've prepared.'

'It's too late for second thoughts, we're committed now.'

'Not until it goes to press. We can pull out any time before.'

'I'll go and see the Pink and if she's willing to co-operate, we'll see the reporters this evening. We can't do anything without her.'

Nini the Pink was delighted. 'How exciting,' she smiled, 'and I'm to be the bait. Pujol, *mon petit*,' she called brightly, 'you can come out now, it's only your Patron, and with such a wonderful idea.'

Pel turned to see Pujol emerge from behind the door. He was blushing and licking his lips in embarrassment.

'What the . . .'

'He's been so sweet,' the Pink explained. 'Took my girls to my sister in Paris, popped in to see me with these beautiful roses and has been looking after me ever since.'

'So that's where you've been.'

'I was working all the time, Patron,' Pujol said, hanging his head and indicating a pile of files on the bedside table.

'In Paris?'

'That was after office hours. It was the least I could do, they were so frightened when I discovered them in the cupboard. After twenty-four hours in the children's ward recovering from the shock they still looked lost and there was no one else, her sister doesn't drive.'

'And the roses?'

'My own money, sir. You told Cheriff to order flowers for Brigitte Breille, we all chipped in to pay for them, so I did the same for Nini, but the protection was my own idea – I was worried he might come back.'

Pel looked the man up and down. He reminded him of himself a hundred years ago – small, not very attractive, his glasses misting up the moment there was any excitement, and too much initiative – but he hadn't got time to tear him off a strip.

'That', he said, 'is precisely what we're planning, but if you don't mind I'll have you replaced by someone tougher.'

*

Finding a small private clinic willing to co-operate wasn't too difficult. Its director hoped it might provide some free publicity when the famous criminal was caught under his roof, and agreed to move his patients round to provide the police with a small but empty ward.

Pel gave Sarrazin, the only trustworthy journalist they knew, the story just before midnight. It had taken that long to organise everything.

'Too late for the morning papers,' he pointed out.

Pel reached for the packet of Gauloises. He was tired and very concerned about what might happen next, he wanted to go home and get a good night's sleep, his lungs were like dirty ashtrays, his stomach was full of gallons of black coffee. Between his indigestion and the caffeine he'd be a wreck in the morning. He sighed, thought better of the cigarette and let the packet drop back on to the desk untouched. 'It's got to be in tomorrow,' he said forcefully. 'Pull strings, call the editors personally – Holy Mother of God, if you decided you wanted to do it, it would be done. I'm asking you, no, pleading with you. We can't risk the wait.'

'Pel pleading?' Sarrazin sneered. 'It's got to be important then.'

24

When Pujol brought the morning papers in to Pel, he was pleased to see Sarrazin had done his stuff: there was a 'Stop Press' on almost every front page.

JC STRIKES AGAIN. Fourth young woman was brutally attacked in Burgundy. Stabbed twelve times, still alive, weak, wanting to talk. 'I know my attacker well,' she said this evening. Police anticipate arrest any day now. At last! Sarrazin (Dijon).

It was exactly as they'd given it to him, except for the final two words and of course his name. The television news at 8 a.m. carried a short item about Nini's anxiety to sell her story to the press. It also included a brief statement to the effect that after a night in the General Hospital, her condition was stable and she was being moved to the Clinique Durand. They quoted her as saying, 'They make better tea.' It would be repeated another three times throughout the day.

It all sounded plausible and genuine. Pel hoped like hell JC was watching for information. He looked up and realised Pujol was still hovering by his desk.

'Yes?' he hissed.

'Please, sir, you haven't appointed me a place at the clinic.'

'Pujol, you and Rigal are on the phones with Misset, I can't afford a couple of new boys or a fool buggering up this operation. Go to your desk and stay there until you're needed to type up the report. And lastly, stop worrying about your girlfriend, she won't be anywhere near the clinic.'

Pujol looked puzzled.

Pel sighed. 'You don't think I'm stupid enough to actually put an innocent member of the public in danger, do you?' he asked patiently. 'I'm not a lunatic, but if you don't go away and stop whimpering I could rapidly turn into one.'

They had had to consider the possibility that JC might strike in a number of places. He'd hurt a lot of people already and if he was intending to finish off one witness as they hoped, why not all of them? He was irrational enough, and now that he was being prompted into action it could start anywhere. Pel deployed part of his team to the protection of Brigitte Breille, Anita Tabeyse and Kate Darcy; he was taking no risks. Brochard was to go to Kate's dressed as a peasant on his father's tractor, Brigitte's brother had turned up in the shape of Bardolle, and Debray, armed with a large bunch of flowers and done up like a Christmas parcel, had a lovers' rendezvous with Anita. But the majority of them were at the clinic in rue de Lorraine.

Cheriff and Nosjean were reclining in Rooms 1 and 5, either side of Nini the Pink's. Darcy was directly opposite in Room 4, sitting in a wheelchair facing a mirror but with his back to the door. Didier Darras was employed as a cleaner pushing his large fluffy mop up and down the corridor, in and out of the rooms. Pel had a stethoscope round his neck and was dressed in white, while the head nurse on the ward was an experienced policewoman borrowed from another team. She did as she was told, playing out her role convincingly. The star turn of Nini the Pink was naturally taken by the only real actor among them, Angelface Aimedieu. Done up in a frilly pink full-length night-dress and appropriate wig, he called for hot tea which Annie, smothering giggles, delivered in her capacity as *aide soignante*. There was no one else on the eight-bedroom ward. All the other convalescing patients had been

172

moved to the two floors above, well behind closed doors. They'd been told nothing and everyone hoped they'd remain ignorant of what was going on until it was over.

But nothing happened. The nurses above went about their work as usual, calmly hiding any anxieties they may have had, but as the clock ticked round again Dr Pel was desperate for a smoke and the rest of his team were growing bored. The only exception was Aimedieu who continued to call for tea; he at least seemed to be enjoying himself, flouncing about and causing a fuss in Room 3.

Just before eight thirty that evening Pujol finished his typing and went out into the dark to climb into his old car. Arriving outside the General Hospital, he switched off the lights, stepped out, shut and locked the door, fastidiously checking the boot as well, and made his way to the main entrance. Pel could stop him taking part in their police operation but he couldn't stop him visiting a friend. And if Nini wasn't at the private clinic she had to be still at the hospital.

He walked casually towards the lift, thinking about Nini. She was a strange lady, but there was something about her that appealed to him. He'd managed to buy six more pink roses which were clutched tightly in his left hand. The other man in the lift eyed them as if the bouquet would leap out and attack him. Pujol thought he recognised him, but that often happened in a policeman's life.

The lift stopped and both men stepped out into the corridor. Pujol hesitated, allowing the other man to go ahead. He went to the desk and asked for the room number of his sister, Nini. The receptionist opened her mouth, remembered something, and looked quickly down at her hidden instructions.

'Ah, no,' she said, 'that patient has been moved to the Clinique Durand.'

'Are you sure?'

'Quite sure, monsieur. She's on the first floor, Room 3.'

Turning back towards the lift Pujol finally saw him full face.

Something flashed. The hair was black not blond but Pujol had studied the files often enough not to be mistaken. He nodded nervously at him and approached the desk. 'I've come to see my mother,' he said. 'She was brought in this afternoon.'

JC was stepping out of sight.

'I was at work when she fell,' Pujol mumbled on while listening for the closing lift doors.

'*Oui, monsieur*, her name please.'

Pujol turned to confirm that JC was really gone.

'It doesn't matter,' he said, ripping his identification out of his pocket. 'I'm a policeman.' He practically threw his wallet at the girl. 'Call the Hôtel de Police immediately and tell Pel, P,E,L, that our man is on his way.'

He turned towards the emergency exit. 'Do it now, please, it's extremely urgent!' He'd left the roses on the desk and called back as he ran, 'Those are for you, compliments of the Police Judiciaire!' before disappearing from sight.

Misset took the call. The receptionist told him Sergeant Pujol had left an urgent message for Pel. The message was, 'The man's on his way.' Misset scratched his head and dialled the number he'd been left with. It was the policewoman who answered.

'Tell Pel there's a message for him from Pujol,' Misset informed her. 'He's on his way.'

'Holy Mother of God!' Pel exploded. 'What does the silly little sod want now?'

He called to Didier Darras, who was still pushing his mop round in circles. 'Get down to the front door. When Pujol comes through it, throw him straight back out again, and tell him he's fired!'

Because Pujol was a young but very conscientious policeman, he had studied the street map of the city for many long hours.

174

While indulging in his evening cruising, he often practised short cuts down back streets most people didn't even know existed and as a result he arrived outside the clinic before JC. He was sure this was the case and, after a quick look up and down the rue de Lorraine, marched through the front door full of confidence – only to be grabbed by the arm and marched smartly straight back into the street again. An unlit van coasted to a halt opposite them. There was a minor scuffle while Darras and Pujol explained themselves. JC silently rolled down his window to listen. The policemen quickly realised the error in the message and were about to bolt for the clinic to inform Pel when Pujol stopped. He was staring after the van which was accelerating away from the kerb.

'Forget it,' he cried, 'that was him,' and dashed off for his own wheels. Fumbling with the keys, he finally gained entry and shot off in hot pursuit while Darras went cantering up the stairs of the clinic.

Pel was furious. 'Our plan worked and now we've lost him again.'

'Pujol's following,' Darras pointed out.

'What good will that do?' Pel bellowed, reaching for his cigarettes. 'His old dustbin doesn't go faster than a pushchair on a fête day.'

Hearing Pel's raised voice, his men came rapidly into the corridor.

'Darcy! Get the description blasted to all police. Tell Pomereu to seal off the city. Tell him it's bloody urgent. Do it on the move. The rest of you, out into the cars and keep your eyes open. Radios tuned to the emergency channel.'

The men started scattering. 'Aimedieu, stay here just in case he comes back. Annie, you stay too as back-up. Go and explain to the nurses upstairs what's happened.'

JC drove at high speed through the city, squealing his tyres round corners and narrowly missing the few night-time pedestrians. His headlights swung from side to side as he sped past dawdling cars. His anger was developing into hate, the headache that went with it piercing his brain. How dare they set a trap? How dare they lie in wait? But they wouldn't catch him, he was too clever.

He screeched through a pair of red lights and wrenched the wheels to the right into a side street. Suddenly he stopped; the needle of pain behind his eyes had turned into a gouging knife. His eyes closed and he buried his head in his hands, kneading his temples with tense fingers.

Pujol had lost him. His old car had tried valiantly to keep up, its engine complaining, but finally it shrieked, gave up and died. He left the steaming wreck and started running. But the van had disappeared. He hadn't a hope, there wasn't a taxi in sight and, searching for his police identification, he remembered he'd left it with the roses at the hospital. He couldn't even commandeer someone else's transport. It was hopeless.

When JC eventually opened his eyes, the cinema on the other side of the road was emptying. Squinting through his pain, he finally made out the title of the film. Filthy *cons*, a blue movie. People disgusted him – revelling in manufactured dirt. As if there wasn't enough in the world without paying to watch it. There were one or two giggling girls among the men. It was revolting, they were the worst. '*Les putes*,' he said out loud and started the engine. He knew where he was going at last, he knew what he had to do.

Pujol didn't. He was jogging. Without an overcoat the biting wind was cutting through his clothes and making him shiver. He had a lot of problems on his mind, a lot of questions he couldn't answer, but running eased his frustration.

Pel arrived in the sergeants' room to wait for news. It had been a complete disaster, once again JC had slipped through their fingers. He stared at Misset, who was slumped behind a desk, and the telephone between them.

'Our only hope', he said to himself, 'is if Pomereu and his boys manage to pick him up on his way out of the city. Where's Pujol got to?'

Misset brightened visibly. 'He rang to say he was on his way,' he said. 'I can't imagine why he's taking so long.'

'Shut up!' Pel shouted. 'Another word out of you and you'll be fired too. Rigal, bring me up to date.'

'No more messages from Pujol, but one from Annie Saxe.' He paused to take a breath.

'Well, don't stop there, tell me, man.'

'All quiet at the clinic.'

'And the other men with Breille, Tabeyse and Kate?'

'Phoned in earlier, nothing to report.'

Pomereu came through the door rubbing his chin and went straight to the street map of the city attached to the wall. 'The road blocks are in place, Pel.' His hand swept round the outside touching the main junctions. 'We set them up well out of the centre where the roads are fewer and because of the time element. He may not have reached the outskirts before we did. The local gendarmeries have been alerted to cover the minor country roads but I can't guarantee their efficiency. They weren't pleased to be disturbed after lights out at six o'clock and grumbled about having to go out.'

'I hope you pointed out the urgency,' Pel demanded.

'I threatened them with the sack, the Préfet and the President.'

'Well done. Marked cars?'

'Twelve, all cruising.'

'Between us we may manage to corner him, get him worried and force him into making a mistake or running for it. I think we may be in with a chance.'

'Unless he's gone to ground or was faster than I thought.'

Their grim silence was broken by the phone. Pel snatched it up before Misset had time to make a nuisance of himself. It was the gendarmerie at Talant. 'Adjudant Lassar *à l'appareil*. We've apprehended your runaway. He's in custody here at the *caserne*.'

25

At last. When Pel arrived in Talant he was delighted and prepared to take back all he'd ever said about slow-witted village policemen. When he left he'd said it all over again but far louder than before. He was furious. He'd fired the entire gendarmerie, commiserated with an innocent electrician who'd been out on a late call and wished him luck with the legal proceedings he was proposing to bring against Lassar, who was curled up in his office licking his wounds.

The hunt was still on.

Pujol had stopped running; he was out of breath and becoming tired. Having been into Centre Ville and run round in circles achieving nothing he was now standing at the end of rue de Lorraine watching the large white clouds of his own breath disperse into the sub-zero night. There were few cars parked in the narrow street; it was almost deserted. Not far away was the green neon light of the Clinique Durand, just beyond was a beige van. There was no driver. He stepped back from the corner, took one more look and within seconds was pounding on the first door he came to.

Inside the clinic, the nurses, relieved it had all come to nothing, had done their rounds, checking that the individual *sonnettes* were connected and carefully tucking everyone in for the night. They were relaxing in their staff room, out of sight from the wards and the patients. No one saw the tall figure insinuate itself through the front door and make its way up the stairs to the first floor.

As the ward door swung open, Annie stood up, swallowed

hard and stepped out from behind the desk. Before she had time to speak JC punched her in the mouth and made his way towards Room 3. Annie was unconscious.

Aimedieu was dozing, but when the hand closed over his mouth his eyes shot open. He was suddenly wide awake. Dragged from his bed and out into the corridor, the curly wig flopping over his eyes and obscuring his view, he still managed to see Annie folded against the wall and knew there was no one to help. A fight now would produce nothing but a lot of blood, his blood. The point of a knife was digging into his side ready to pierce through flesh and internal organs alike. Locked together like honeymooners they went slowly down the stairs. By the large front door JC prepared for their exit; he bought the knife up to Aimedieu's throat, then released his mouth to grab his hair.

He gasped, staring at the wig in his hand.

It was Aimedieu's chance. His elbow came back violently below JC's ribs, stealing his breath and doubling him up. Aimedieu spun round and, kneeing him hard in the groin, swung his fist to finish the affair. But JC saw it coming.

He staggered to the right, and Aimedieu missed. Instead he felt the full pain as JC smashed him in the kidneys. He hit the floor, where JC kicked him savagely in the ribs several times. Aimedieu curled into a ball and was kicked in the head. Balls of fire exploded in his brain, his eyes wouldn't focus, he was fighting to regain control of himself.

JC did it for him: he hauled him almost to his feet and roughly dragged him towards the large front door, but Aimedieu was a dead weight at the end of his arms.

From his position behind a parked car, Pujol watched as the torn pink night-dress tumbled from the pavement into the road. The van was a few paces away. The night-dress struggled to its knees, to be knocked down again by the crazed JC.

Sirens were heard. JC looked wild-eyed about him then, grabbing Aimedieu's limp body, he backed up towards the clinic.

Annie fell down the last of the stairs, crawled to the front door and on all fours peeped out. The sirens were getting closer, so was JC. With all her strength she rose to a standing position, reached for the large bolts and collapsed.

Cornered like a rat. The door to the clinic wouldn't open. There were blinding headlights at either end of the street and nothing but a row of empty shops and offices in front of him. JC dragged Aimedieu back out into the road. The occupants of the two police cars watched in horror. The pink night-dress was pulled into a sitting position, bare white feet sticking up from lifeless legs, arms hanging limply, head lolling. JC grabbed it and tilted it back, exposing the throat and placing his knife against the prominent Adam's apple. He screamed into the lights.

'Come near me and I'll slit her throat from ear to ear.'

In one of the cars Darcy and Nosjean listened to the threat. 'My God,' Darcy said, 'he still thinks it's a woman.'

'Confused. Keep him calm while I find Pel.' Nosjean reached for the car phone.

'Tell him to bring the troops and to hurry, it's looking dangerous. Aimedieu may already be past help,' Darcy added, climbing out to stand unseen behind the glare of the car's lights.

'Okay, JC, we heard you, don't cut her,' he shouted. 'We're prepared to negotiate. What do you want?'

'I want to be left alone. Go away and leave me alone.'

'We can't do that,' Nosjean said quietly at Darcy's side.

'Where's Pel?'

'On his way. That's Cheriff, Darras and the borrowed policewoman at the other end of the street. Keep him talking.'

'Hang on a minute, will you, mate,' Darcy shouted back. 'I've got to confer with the boss.'

'How long will Pel be?' he asked Nosjean. 'This is a dead-end conversation.'

'Five minutes, maybe ten, he's coming from Talant.'

'I might keep it up until then.'

Turning back towards the sad scene in the street, Darcy

raised his voice again. 'Anyone you'd like to talk to in the meantime?'

JC lifted a hand to raise one finger in the direction of the headlights, letting Aimedieu's head flop to one side.

'Did you see that?' Darcy whispered.

'I think so,' Nosjean agreed cautiously. 'Aimedieu winked.'

As JC's hand came back down to retrieve the flopping head, Aimedieu snapped his arms together, bunched his hands into a ball and brought them up viciously towards JC's face. He caught him on the chin. It was enough to knock him off balance, but that was all. The next moment he was on his feet, the lights glinting off the cold sharp blade of his knife as it came swooping down towards the pink night-dress.

'Move!' Darcy screamed, and all five police officers threw themselves down the hundred metres towards the murderous rapist. They seemed like miles.

From the shadows a body hurled itself at the cutting arm. It collided with the broad shoulders and JC fell flat on his face, spread-eagled across a gasping Aimedieu. But the knife rose again and as it did Pujol sprang up, grabbed the arm and broke it neatly over his knee. The knife clattered into the road.

Aimedieu crawled from beneath the sobbing prisoner and looked up at Pujol who was fiddling with a broken pair of glasses between shaking fingers.

'*Merci, mon vieux,*' he said. 'I owe you.'

JC was shrieking at the top of his voice. 'Call for a doctor, I'm in pain, that bastard broke my fucking arm. How dare you hurt me!'

Pujol slipped his specs into a convenient pocket while looking down at the pathetic rapist, then slowly bending over he took him gently by the hair and banged his head briskly on the tarmac. There was a resounding crack, then sudden blissful silence.

'I say,' Darcy grinned as he came to a halt, 'that wasn't really necessary.'

'But at least he's not waking the entire clinic,' Pujol replied seriously. 'Where's the Patron?'

'Here.' A small solid figure loomed up out of the shadows.

'I think we've caught your criminal, sir.'

'Pujol, you shouldn't be here,' Pel said slowly. 'You were told to stay away and not to interfere. I'll want a complete explanation. In the meantime,' he added lowering his voice, 'the moment he comes round, read him his rights and book him for robbery, rape, grievous bodily harm and attempted murder. He's your arrest. *Félicitations.*'

While they stood over the unconscious JC, a young nurse came running across the road towards them. Coming downstairs with an urgent message she'd found Annie in a heap and, stooping to see how she could help, had heard the noise outside. She'd watched the fight and was still not sure it was safe to be out there. However, it was urgent and she forced herself into the circle of police. It wasn't easy. 'Excuse me,' she insisted, 'but I've a message from Maternité at the hospital. Is Monsieur Nosjean, Jean-Luc, among you? His wife's asking for him.'

'What is it?' Nosjean had gone white.

'Your wife's haemorrhaged again. They've taken her down to the operating theatre.'

Calm and collected until now, Nosjean crumpled. 'Oh my God, Patron!'

'Get going man, we'll cope.'

26

As Nosjean left with his siren blaring, Pel looked Aimedieu up and down. 'Pink doesn't suit you,' he said. 'For the love of God, go and get dressed.'

Annie limped out, holding an ice pack over her mouth. Pel was about to order her back to Casualty when she stopped him. 'I'm all right, sir, just need a broad shoulder to cry on,' she mumbled and shuffled off to the waiting Cheriff.

After his arm had been plastered, JC was escorted to a high security police van, where two armed guards watched him closely throughout the short journey to 72 rue Auxonne, which was what they lovingly called the local prison. Pomereu was informed; he called in his men and the gendarmes. At last everyone was heading for bed. Except Pel, and Pujol, who was wondering how to get home. Pel came up behind him puffing like an old steam train. Now that it was all over, his nerves were jumping about in true French style but another ten thousand Gauloises would see to that. Pujol had behaved bravely and was looking lost. The young man strangely saluted his boss and ambled off in the hope of finding a taxi.

'Where do you think you're going,' Pel snapped, 'because I'm taking you. Without your glasses you're as blind as a bat, I don't want to have to send out a search party for you later. The evening's been long enough already.'

Pujol followed him to his car and wearily climbed in.

'You're a disobedient little bugger, aren't you?' Pel said. 'You weren't supposed to be anywhere near the clinic tonight.'

'I was off duty and visiting a friend at the hospital,' Pujol explained. 'JC was there asking for Nini. I followed him here then I followed him half-way round the city until my car blew up, so I took off on foot and discovered the van back here. I phoned for help and hid. I was terrified,' he added quietly, 'and now I can't seem to stop shaking.'

'Don't worry, you'll get over it,' Pel reassured him.

At Pujol's request, Pel drove him to the General Hospital and escorted him to Nini the Pink's bedside. She was still awake and sipping at the inevitable cup of tea.

They recounted the events of the evening, Nini's eyes growing wider all the time and her hold on Pujol's hand ever tighter.

'As I was saying,' Pel concluded, 'you're a disobedient little bugger, but I suppose there's no need for disciplinary action,' he added begrudgingly. 'Come on, if we can find a bar still open, I'll buy you a drink.'

'Thank you, sir, but I'd rather stay here a while.'

Pel left them to it. He smoked the rest of his Gauloises on the way home, trying to catch up on what he'd missed during his time at the clinic and thinking ominously of all the paperwork he'd have to do the following morning. Rigal would be chained to the typewriter for weeks.

The morning meeting was more pleasant than usual. De Troq' had sorted out the Brazilian police and was due back in Paris any day accompanied by a refortified mother and a sister carrying at least one spare anvil in her handbag. Annie's mouth was badly swollen but she managed a smile when Aimedieu, sporting his voluptuous wig, acted out the final scene of the arrest for those who hadn't been there. Clutching at his bruised body he bowed dramatically as Pel opened the door. The applause stopped instantly as he scowled at the lot of them. But on the whole it was good news, he only threatened to fire half the team.

'Don't think we've finished – what about the other Bonnet

murder?' he yelled gently. 'Roger, who was rotting under five tonnes of logs – what have you done about that?'

'Some people are never satisfied,' Misset muttered as he was leaving.

'And you, Misset,' Pel retorted, 'can go back for another operation any time you like. Let's hope it's terminal this time.'

The door slammed. Darcy looked at his boss: he was grinning. It was enough to frighten Frankenstein.

Pel pestered Cham and Boudet in desperation – surely they could come up with something on the Roger Bonnet case? – but their inspiration had run dry. Cham was still unable to tell him what he'd been hit with. That seemed to be the key to the case and the one thing no one could determine. Pel paced round his office, his brain in top gear but bringing no results. He was going to have to take it out on someone. As usual he headed for the sergeants' room.

Most of his men were there, all of them looking busy. He stood with his hands on his hips wondering which one to pick on. Misset was the obvious choice but that was getting boring. Pujol didn't deserve it today. Rigal was typing Pel's lengthy report of JC's arrest, he could hardly interrupt him.

Nosjean wandered in looking worried.

'Well?' Pel asked turning on him.

'I'm a father,' he replied, looking shell-shocked. 'I saw it all. The baby turned round at the last minute and they didn't have to operate, it was a normal birth. God, it was grim.'

The sergeants' room collapsed into laughter. Pel slipped out. Baby talk contained vocabulary that was beyond him.

During the afternoon he called Nosjean to his office. 'Congratulations,' he said, handing him a bottle of champagne. 'Now sod off back to your wife and child and stop looking so worried – it's happened before, you know.'

Pel was feeling weary as he drove home that night; a lot had happened and there was no doubt a lot more to come. For once he'd left on time and was looking forward to a quiet evening at home with his wife. If necessary he'd tie and gag Madame Routy to a kitchen chair. Tonight he was not going to be disturbed.

When he arrived, however, he was unable to park his car in the drive; an ambulance was blocking the entrance. Sighing, he left the car in the road and stamped up the path to meet two SAMU men carrying Madame Routy out. His wife was following them.

'What happened?' he asked. 'Did you finally manage to have her committed?'

'She was messing about with a piece of frozen pork and dropped it on her foot,' his wife explained in a whisper. 'I think she's broken a toe.'

Pel didn't stop smiling all evening. And a good night's sleep to come . . . But it was not to be.

27

Half-way through his restless dreams he woke suddenly. 'My God!' he said. 'Of course!' He was so convinced he was right he didn't sleep another wink and was ready to leave for work exhausted at six o'clock the next morning. His wife kissed him goodbye and went back to bed.

When Dr Cham arrived in his office at eight, Pel had already filled the room with smoke. He listened carefully to what Pel had to suggest then went to his files.

'It's possible,' he agreed after studying the report he'd made on the head wound of Roger Bonnet. 'Yes, it's possible. That's why we couldn't work out what the murder weapon was – it doesn't exist any more.'

'I've a lot of checking to do,' Pel pointed out. 'It's just an idea, as you and Boudet are so fond of saying.'

He left Cham and went to his own office, calling for Nosjean and Darcy.

'Good morning,' he said cheerfully. They looked at one another wondering what bomb he was about to drop. 'How's the little one?' he asked Nosjean. 'Mother and child doing well, I trust?'

'Yes, thank you, they're absolutely fine.'

'And Kate, recuperating nicely?'

'Slowly but surely, yes.'

'And the dog?'

'True to his name,' Darcy confirmed, wondering where his boss was leading them. 'It takes more than a bullet wound to kill Rasputin.'

'Take a seat,' Pel went on, offering them both a cigarette, a sickly smile still sitting on his face.

Once they were all alight, Pel pulled a single fat file towards him. It was the Roger Bonnet file.

'I've been reading this through,' he told them, 'as I hope you have. Darcy, I know you didn't go with Nosjean to interview Claudine Bonnet, but as my second-in-command you should know the file off by heart.'

Darcy nodded doubtfully. It felt like a trap.

Pel let the smile drop. 'I think at last I've cracked it, but I'd like you to answer a few questions before I close this file forever.'

Again Darcy and Nosjean exchanged glances but said nothing; they puffed silently on their cigarettes and awaited interrogation.

'We'll start at the beginning, shall we? Claudine said she had gone to the garage to collect something from the freezer when she heard her husband arrive outside with his secretary. Correct?'

They nodded.

'She was furious at the conversation and kissing she heard and went to greet him on the garden path. She said she slapped him. What were she and her relations eating when you interviewed her the following day?'

'I don't think I remember.'

'I do,' Nosjean admitted. 'It was a *gigot d'agneau* and it was revolting. I've never seen a family attack a meal with such gusto.'

'Never mind the gusto, it's the leg of lamb I'm interested in. She would have got it out of the freezer the night before to defrost, *n'est-ce pas*?'

They nodded. Being domesticated men they knew all about defrosting meat slowly.

'I think that's what killed Roger Bonnet. Claudine went to the freezer to extract the leg of lamb, overheard her husband with his secretary, came out to greet him holding it in her hand. She didn't slap him, she hit him with something as hard as a piece of lead piping and weighing as much, three kilos of frozen lamb. She turned and went inside. He staggered out through the garden gate and fell alongside the fence. It was snowing gently, remember, just enough to cover the ground.'

'And the body,' Darcy said, seeing the light.

'Precisely. The woodman delivered his wood shortly afterwards, about seven o'clock, he said. He reversed his tractor and trailer up towards their gate, he couldn't possibly have seen the body, particularly if it was covered in snow. He dumped his load, went in to be paid and left. *Et violà!*'

'And the next day I watched Claudine and her revolting relations eat the murder weapon.' Nosjean was incredulous.

'What does Cham say?' Darcy asked cautiously.

'He's busy trying to prove it. I expect by the end of the morning to have his confirmation,' Pel said smugly and, flamboyantly flipping the file closed, he succeeded in scattering its contents all over the floor.

It had been a good day. Cham had delivered the necessary proof, having experimented with a similar lump of frozen lamb. Pel was well pleased – only the other million cases to clear now, nothing he couldn't do in his spare time. As he scrambled into his heavy overcoat there was a knock at the door.

It was Pujol, as usual licking his lips nervously and carrying a hefty file.

'Oh, no, what do you want? In fact don't tell me, I'm going home. The dragon Routy has been detained and I'm going to spend another peaceful evening with my wife.'

'Sorry, sir, but it's the cock problem,' Pujol replied, standing his ground. 'I thought you'd like to know.'

'If the neighbour's shot the farmer, arrest him, and if the farmer's shot the neighbour, shake his ruddy hand for me. I'm still going home.'

Pujol went on regardless. 'They went to court and the

farmer lost. The cock was considered to be a public nuisance and the farmer would be ordered to pay compensation if it continued to crow at the weekend.'

'Incredible.'

'The farmer's wife made it into *coq au vin*. I took Nini to celebrate with them.'

'Celebrate what, the death of a poor bloody cock?'

'No, sir. I discovered a *droit de passage* that exists since before the land was sold for building houses on. He has the right of way straight across their front gardens and he's using it. He drives his herd of cows across it twice a day, once in the morning after milking to take them to the pasture beyond, and again later to bring them in for the evening milking. At the moment it's just shit shock they're suffering from, but when the flies get going in the summer they won't be able to stroke their gnomes for the infestation.'

'Go home!' Pel bellowed, but he was almost smiling again.